HENRYK SIENKIEWICZ:
THREE STORIES

HENRYK SIENKIEWICZ:
THREE STORIES

TRANSLATED BY

PETER J. OBST

WILDSIDE PRESS

Published by Wildside Press LLC.
www.wildsidebooks.com

DEDICATED TO

BERNHARDT BLUMENTHAL

1937 - 2012

SCHOLAR, EDUCATOR, MOTIVATOR

HIERSEIN IST HERRLICH

SIC TRANSIT GLORIA MUNDI

CONTENTS

Henryk Sienkiewicz 9

Works by Henryk Sienkiewicz. 15

A Comedy of Errors 17

The Authoresses 39

The Third One 53

Commentary on The Third One 115

HENRYK SIENKIEWICZ

Sienkiewicz was born on May 5, 1846 into an impoverished noble family in the village of Wola Okrzejska. At first, his father rented various manor lands, then settled in Warsaw where he purchased an apartment house. Sienkiewicz finished high school in Warsaw and attended university there from 1866 to 1871, where he studied law and philology-history. He finished his studies in 1871 but never received his diploma, for he skipped his exam in the Greek language.

In his youth, Sienkiewicz was inspired by the high-spirited adventure in the stories of Alexandre Dumas. When the unsuccessful uprising against Russian domination broke out in January 1863, his parents refused him permission to participate, since his older brother Kazimierz (who would later die in the Franco-Prussian War) had already gone to fight. Disappointed, he concentrated on Poland's past glories and family history. His first youthful forays into literature were poetry and a novel of student life—*Na Marne (In Vain)*—which received some critical praise.

From 1872 to 1887, Sienkiewicz worked as a journalist and reporter for the Warsaw press, and by 1874 he became co-owner of the bi-weekly *Niwa,* remaining in that position until 1878. In 1876 he was sent as a correspondent to North America by *Gazeta Polska.* Simultaneously, he was the advanceman for a group of friends, including the actress Helena Modrzejewska (later Modjeska), who were intent on resettling in the United States, and he half-heartedly joined their attempt to start a communal farm in Anaheim, California. He stayed only until 1878.

In 1879 he traveled through France and Italy, and after 1880 he traveled constantly. Every year he made trips abroad so that his first wife, Maria Szetkiewicz, could receive treatment for her tuberculosis. In addition to his travels, he was the editor of *Słowo* (a conservative daily) between 1882 and 1887. After his first wife's death in 1885, he frequented spas in Austria, Italy, and France. In 1886 he ventured further afield, to Constantinople, Athens, Naples, and Rome. Spain was his destination in 1888, and in 1890 Sienkiewicz joined a hunting expedition to Zanzibar.

He was a tireless traveler and wrote continuously, producing novels, short stories, commentaries, and letters, which appeared in the press in Krakow, Warsaw, Poznan, and Lwow. The work brought him fame. In 1900, on the 25th anniversary of his writing debut, a grateful nation presented him with Oblęgorek, a small estate with a manor house near Kielce (in southeastern Poland).

He received the Nobel Prize for Literature in 1905. By giving the prize to a "Polish writer," the Swedish Academy recognized the language of a country that, at that time, did not exist as a nation-state. Poland had been partitioned out of existence in 1795, and its lands remained under the control of Prussia, Russia, and Austria until 1918 and the end of World War I. In his address to the Academy,[1] Sienkiewicz said:

---

1   From *Nobel Lectures, Literature 1901-1967*, Editor Horst Frenz, Elsevier Publishing Company, Amsterdam, 1969.

Nations are represented by their poets and their writers in the open competition for the Nobel Prize. Consequently the award of the Prize by the Academy glorifies not only the author but the people whose son he is, and it bears witness that that nation has a share in the universal achievement, that its efforts are fruitful, and that it has the right to live for the profit of mankind. If this honour is premous to all, it is infinitely more so to Poland. It has been said that Poland is dead, exhausted, enslaved, but here is the proof of her life and triumph. Like Galileo, one is forced to think "E pur si muove"[2] when before the eyes of the world homage has been rendered to the importance of Poland's achievement and her genius.

This homage has been rendered not to me—for the Polish soil is fertile and does not lack better writers than me—but to the Polish achievement, the Polish genius. For this I should like to express my most ardent and most sincere gratitude as a Pole to you gentlemen, the members of the Swedish Academy, and I conclude by borrowing the words of Horace: "Principibus placuisse viris non ultima laus est."[3]

After the outbreak of World War I, Sienkiewicz moved to Vevey, Switzerland where, with Ignacy Jan Paderewski and A. Osuchowski, he organized the General Committee to Help the Victims of War in Poland. The committee sent medicine, clothing, and money to their beleaguered homeland. Sienkiewicz also joined other social relief efforts, including the creation of a tuberculosis treatment center for children in Bystre. A fund for writers, which he founded in 1889, helped Stanisław Wyspiański, Stanisław Przybyszewski, K. Przerwa-Tetmayer, and many others

---

2   "and yet it moves"
3   "to have won the approval of important people is not the last degree of praise"

to spend time in sanatoriums. He died in Vevey on November 15, 1916 of a heart aliment.

Sienkiewicz traveled extensively throughout his later life, and met many interesting people. He married Maria Szetkiewicz (1881), with whom he had two children: Henryk Józef and Jadwiga. Despite visits to spas for the rest cure, the only treatment then available, Maria died from tuberculosis in 1885. His subsequent marriage to Maria Romanowska-Wołodkiewicz, which he admitted was an error in judgment, was annulled on technical grounds. Later, in 1904, he married Maria Babska, who became his true partner for the rest of their lives.

Testimony to his wide interests is given by his extensive travel reports: *Letters from America* and *Letters from Africa*. In his writings on Polish themes he addressed contemporary social problems, the poverty of the villages, and the oppression in schools operated under the occupation government. In his cycle of short stories written about America, he illustrated life in that young and resilient nation. With over 40 major works, he displayed his mastery of the Polish language, human psychology, and the writer's craft. Sienkiewicz was instrumental in the flowering of the historical novel at the end of the nineteenth century; he was a writer with a historical temperament. His contemporary novels *Without Dogma (Bez Dogmatu)* and *The Polaniecki Family (Rodzina Połanieckich)* were not successful, but his historical novels brought him worldwide fame. His greatest success was *Quo Vadis*, a great panoramic portrayal of Nero's Rome. The first part of his *Trilogy—With Fire and Sword (Ogniem i Mieczem)*—raised him to the level of the greatest Polish prose writers.

Literary and academic circles initially criticized the *Trilogy*, accusing Sienkiewicz of a lack of understanding for human psychology, and asserting that the novels did not present an accurate historical picture of events. Despite this, the *Trilogy* instantly became the most popular books in Poland and quickly gained admirers overseas. The *Trilogy* was written chiefly to "uplift the hearts" of his countrymen, and taught patriotism and faith in individual heroism.

The crowning success of his work was the novel *The Teutonic Knights (Krzyżacy)*. The epic nature of the story, its well-organized action sequences, and the presentation of a growing national awareness testify to its great artistic and imaginative values. Among young people, his novel of Africa was a great favorite: *In Desert and Wilderness (W Pustyni i w Puszczy)*.

According to bibliographer and Sienkiewicz scholar Julian Krzyżanowski, Sienkiewicz remains among the world's most popular writers. Sienkiewicz's works are continually reprinted or appear in new translations. In the United States, the *Trilogy* and *Quo Vadis* received a new treatment in the 1990s with English language versions by author-translator Wieslaw Kuniczak. These works quickly became controversial among veteran Sienkiewicz readers because of the adaptive approach used in producing these new editions. Kuniczak's critics said that he crossed the line from translation to co-authorship.[4] On the other hand, his defenders held that everything was done in the "spirit of" the original novels to make them

---

4   Harold B. Segel, book review in *The Polish Review* XXXVI, No. 4, (1991), p. 487; Michael J. Mikoś, book review in *The Polish Review* XXXVII, 2, (1992), p. 253.

"more accessible" to a new and wider English-speaking readership.[5]

Yet despite any controversy, the first book of the series, *With Fire and Sword*, quickly became a Book of the Month selection. This is ample evidence that Sienkiewicz continues to speak across time even to readers outside of Poland. He is gone. The centennial of his Nobel Prize in Literature has passed. Yet his unique vision of history, expressed with great narrative skill, continues to engage and fascinate readers willing to make the effort to know him.

Biographical sketch information from:

Borowiec, Jerzy. *Encyclopedyczny Słownik Sławnych Polaków* [*An Encyclopedic Directory of Famous Poles*], Warsaw: Oficyna Wydawniczo-Poligraficzna i Reklamowo Handlowa "Adam," 1996.

* * * *

---

5   *The Trilogy Companion: A Reader's Guide to the Trilogy of Henryk Sienkiewicz*, Jerzy R. Krzyżanowski, ed., (New York: Copernicus Society of America and Hippocrene Books, 1991).

WORKS BY HENRYK SIENKIEWICZ

Letters from America	1876-1878	
Letters from Africa	1891-1892	
On a Single Card	1879	stage play
On Naturalism in the Novel	1880	literary critique
On the Historical Novel	1889	literary critique
Letters about Zola	1893	a study

SHORT STORIES/NOVELLAS

Humor from Worszala's Portfolio	1872	
The Old Servant	1875	*Stary Sługa*
Hania	1875	
Charcoal Sketches	1877	*Szkice Węglem*
Selim Mirza	1877	
Janko Musician	1879	*Janko Muzykant*
For Bread	1880	*Za Chlebem*
Orso	1880	
Across the Steppes	1880	*Przez Stepy*
The Lighthouse Keeper	1881	*Latarnik*
Jamiol	1882	
Bartek the Victor	1882	*Bartek Zwycięsca*
Sachem	1889	
A Reminiscence from Mariposa	1889	*Wspomnienie z Maripozy*
The Third One	1889	*Ta Trzecia*
Sabala's Tale	1889	*Sabałowa Bajka*

NOVELS

For Naught	1872	*Na Marne*
The Trilogy:		
With Fire and Sword	1883-1884	*Ogniem i Mieczem*
The Deluge	1886	*Potop*
Colonel Wolodyjowski	1888	*Pan Wołodyjowski*
Without Dogma	1890	*Bez Dogmatu*
The Polaniecki Family	1894	*Rodzina Połanieckich*
Quo Vadis	1896	
The Teutonic Knights	1900	*Krzyżacy*
On the Field of Glory	1903-1905	*Na Polu Chwały*
Whirlpools	1910	*Wiry*
In Desert and Wilderness	1911	*W Pustyni i w Puszczy*
Legions	1914	*Legiony*

A COMEDY OF ERRORS

SKETCH FROM AMERICAN LIFE (1876)

INTRODUCTION

Whether the incident which serves as the core of the following sketch took place in the east or in the west, I could not find out. But really it does not matter. It is also possible that some American or German novelist used it already, which in my opinion also should make no difference to the readers, along with the name of the town.

Using an author's license I tell the story as if it happened in California. At the same time I will try to give a few characteristic glimpses into small-town life there.

* * * *

This happened five or six years ago, in Mariposa County when in a certain locality there was discovered a source of crude oil. The huge profits that may be had from extraction of minerals in Nevada and other states quickly mobilized a few entrepreneurs to create a company to exploit this newly discovered resource. Soon, various pieces of machinery, pumps, derricks, ladders, barrels and drums, drills and boilers were brought in. Houses were built for workers and the place was christened with the name Struck Oil. In short order, in this empty and unpopulated locality, which belonged to the coyotes a year earlier, stood a settlement composed of a few dozen houses occupied by several hundred workers.

Two years later Struck Oil became Struck Oil City. And it was a city in the full meaning of the word. After all, there was a shoemaker, a tailor, a carpenter, a blacksmith and a French "doctor" who during his time in France shaved many a beard. But he was a "learned" man and harmless, which is much to say about any doctor in America.

The doctor, as it often happens in small towns, was the druggist and the post-master. Thus his practice was three-fold. As a druggist he was also harmless. He only had two medicines: peppermint and licorice. This quite elderly gentleman would tell his patients: "Do not fear my medications. It is my custom that when I prescribe to the sick I also take an equal portion myself for if it will not harm me, a well man, then it will not hurt a sick man either."

"True," said the satisfied citizens, who did not give much thought to the fact that a doctor's duty was not only to do no harm to the patient, but to make him well.

Mr. Dasonville, as was the doctor's name, believed in the wonderful properties of licorice. Often at town meetings he took off his hat and, turning to the audience, said: "Ladies and gentlemen! See what a wonder licorice is! I am seventy years old, for forty years I have been taking licorice daily and notice—there is not one gray hair on my head!"

The ladies and gentlemen could then plainly see that the doctor did not have a single gray hair, but he also had none at all for his head was a bald as the outer surface of a glass lamp globe. However, since any remarks on the subject would not have had a positive contribution to the development of Struck Oil City, no one made any.

Meanwhile, Struck Oil City continued to grow and grow. After two years the railroad ran a spur line to the town. The town had its own elected officers. The good doctor, who was liked universally and was a member of the educated class, became the justice of the peace. The shoemaker, a Polish Jew, Mr. Davis (David) was elected sheriff to head a police department consisting of one person—himself. A school was built and given into the charge of a school marm, an old maid forever suffering from gumboils, who was especially imported for this purpose. Finally, a hotel was built and given the name "United States Hotel."

Business was lively. The sale of kerosene brought in tremendous profits. It was soon noticed that Mr. Davis had a glass show window, not unlike those in San Francisco, built into the front of his store. At the next town meeting the citizens made a public show of gratitude for the addition of "a fine new adornment to the town," to which Mr. Davis replied with great humility. "Thank you, thank you! Oy, vey!"

Where there is a sheriff and a justice of the peace, there must be court cases. This in turn requires record keeping and paper. Thus on the corner of Coyote and First Streets a stationary store was established. There were sold the latest publications including political journals and satirical cartoons showing, for example, President Grant as a farmer milking a cow, which represented the United States. The sheriff did nothing about such things, as censorship lay well outside of his duties.

But that was not the end of it. Any self-respecting American town must have a newspaper of its own. After the second year of its existence there was established a periodical *The Saturday Weekly Review* which had as many subscribers as there were inhabitants in Struck Oil City. The editor of this periodical was its publisher, printer, administrator, and distributor. This last job came all that much easier as he kept cows and each morning delivered milk to the homes of his subscribers. And he had no problem with starting his editorials with the following words: "Had the villainous president of these United States followed the advice which we printed in the last issue then…" And so on.

There was nothing lacking in the blessed environs of Struck Oil City. In addition, the miners who labored to extract crude oil were not noted for their violent behavior or the bad habits that afflicted those who went out to search for gold, so the town had peace. There were no fist fights, lynching was unheard of. Life flowed peacefully, one day was as like to the other as two drops of water. In the morning each man started about his business, in the evening the citizens burned trash in the streets. If there was no town meeting that night, then they could rest easy knowing that on the following evening they would again be burning trash in the streets.

One of the sheriff's main worries was the fact that he could not stop the citizenry from taking pot shots at the wild geese which flew over the town in the evening. The city statutes forbade the discharge of firearms within city limits. "If this was some backward village," mused the sheriff, "then I would not be concerned, but in such a fine town—bang, bang, bang—this is most unlovely."

The citizens listened to his admonitions, nodded their heads and said "Oh, yes! Definitely!" But when the gray and white flocks appeared against the red evening glow, everyone forgot about their resolve and the fusillade began all over again.

Of course Sheriff Davis could have each one of them appear before the justice of the peace, and the justice of the peace could issue a stiff fine, but these same guilty parties were the doctor's patients and, when their heels wore down, also the customers of the shoe maker. Since one hand washes the other—then they do no harm to their opposite.

Thus passed the halcyon days in Struck Oil City—yet, they were soon to end.

The male general store owner started to burn with deathly hate toward his competitor—a woman general store operator.

Here one should explain what is a general store in America. A grocery or general store is an emporium where one can purchase most everything. One can buy flour, hats, cigars, brooms, buttons, rice, sardines, shirts, hog back fat, seeds, jackets, trousers, kerosene lamps, axes, biscuits, plates, paper collars, dried fish—in a word, everything that a person may need. In the beginning there was only one general store in Struck Oil City. It was operated by a German, Hans Kasche by name. He was a phlegmatic individual, born in Prussia. Thirty-five years old, he had bulging eyes, was not fat but somewhat stout, and always went about without a jacket and with a pipe clenched between his teeth. His knowledge of English was just barely sufficient to carry on the business, and that was about all. He was a capable merchant and after a year it was bandied about Struck Oil City that he "was worth" several thousand dollars.

Suddenly, however, a second general store opened.

And a strange thing too! The first one was operated by a German, the second was operated by a German woman. "Kunegunde und Eduard, Eduard und Kunegunde!" so went the song. Soon disputes broke out between these two, and it began at the very arrival of Ms. Laura Neuman. She decided to give a party and served cakes baked of flour mixed with soda and alum. This would have damaged her reputation among the townsfolk had she not been able to prove with witnesses that her own flour had not yet arrived and she had to buy supplies from Hans Kasche. It was apparent from the start that Hans was a jealous and unprincipled competitor who at the very start tried to damage Ms. Neuman's public opinion. It was rather obvious that these two stores would become rivals, but no one expected that this rivalry would contain such a strong element of personal vindictiveness. The vindictiveness advanced to such a degree that Hans would burn trash only when the wind blew in the direction of his competitor's store entrance. Ms. Neuman on the other hand called her opponent Deutsche mann (German) which he took to be the greatest of insults.

At the beginning the townsfolk laughed at them both, especially in that neither could speak good English. Slowly, through their daily interaction with the merchants, two groups emerged, one siding with Hans—the other with Laura. These two camps looked at each other askance and this may have led to the disruption of the general happiness and peace in the community of Struck Oil City, causing grave complications in the future. Mr. Davis, well versed in politics, tried to heal the problem at the source by attempting to broker a peace between the two German immigrants. It would happen that he stood in the middle of the street and spoke to them both in their native language:

"Well, are you going to continue this quarrel? Do you not buy your shoes at the same shoemaker? I've got some nice ones, in all of San Francisco you'll find none better."

"You can't sell shoes to him who soon will be walking barefoot," Ms. Neuman would interrupt sourly.

"And I don't use my legs to bring in customers," Hans would reply in his phlegmatic way.

And it should be told that Ms. Neuman, though German, indeed had a beautiful set of legs, thus such comments filled her heart with deathly disdain.

In town the two camps already started to discuss the matter at the town meetings, but as in America no one can win in a quarrel where a woman is involved, most backed the interests of Ms. Neuman.

Soon Hans noticed that his store was making hardly any profit. But then Ms. Neuman's business was hardly booming, because most of the women in town were on Hans' side. They had noticed that their husbands too often went to make purchases at her store, and took way too long to come back.

When neither store had any customers, Hans and Ms. Neuman would stand in their respective doorways, giving each other looks that could kill. Ms. Neuman then would sing to the tune of *Mein lieber Augustin*.

"Deutsche mann, Deutsche mann, De—Deutsche mann—Deutsche mann, —mann!

Hans would look first at her legs, then at her figure— as if he were examining a week old coyote carcass—then bursting out in a hellish laughter would shout "Mein Gott!"

The intense dislike that boiled in this rather phlegmatic man rose to such a degree that when he went out and found that Ms. Neuman was not at her door he would go about as if he had lost something.

The quarrel would have probably gotten a lot fiercer and found its way to court earlier had it not been that Hans was sure he was fated to lose, especially since Ms. Neuman had the backing of the editor of the *Weekly Saturday Review*.

Hans found out about this quite quickly when he put out the rumor that Ms. Neuman padded her figure. This was not at all unlikely, as in America this is a fairly popular custom. During the following week the *Saturday Weekly Review* carried a thundering article where the editor, making general references to the insults by *Deutsche* men finished with the happy news announcing that he had it on the best authority that the figure of the lady in question needed no padding.

From then on Hans drank his morning coffee black, as he would not buy any cream from the said editor, while Ms. Neuman ordered a double portion. In addition she had the tailor make her a dress whose design left no doubt in convincing everyone that Hans was a liar.

In the face of such female cunning Hans felt utterly defenseless. Meanwhile, Ms. Neuman would come out of her shop, stand at the door and sing even louder.

"Deutsche mann, Deutsche mann, De—Deutsche mann—Deutsche mann, —mann!"

"What can I do?" though Hans. "I could feed some poisoned grain to her chickens—no—she'd take me to court and I'd have to pay. Oh, I know what to do."

That evening, Ms. Neuman, to her great surprise, noticed that Hans was carrying great bunches of sunflowers and laying them out along a pathway the led to the barred window of his cellar.

"I wonder what this is all about," she thought, "probably some trick he's trying to play on me!"

Meanwhile, it got dark. Hans lined up the sunflowers in rows, leaving the center as a pathway to the cellar window. Then he came back with some object wrapped in canvas. This mysterious object he lay down as he turned his back toward Ms. Neuman, then covered it with the sunflower leaves and started to write something on the wall.

Ms. Neuman was overcome by curiosity. "He's probably writing something against me," she thought. "Once everyone is asleep I'll go to see what it is, even if I had to die."

Hans finished his work, went inside and soon put out the light. Then Ms. Neuman threw on her robe, put on her slippers and walked across the street. Reaching the sunflowers she followed the path right to the wall to see what was written there. Suddenly her eyes popped out, her body wrenched into a vertical position, and from her lips came a painful, "Ay, ay!" Then she started to shout, "Help! Help!"

A window flew open upstairs. "Was is das?" said Hans calmly. "Was is das?"

"You rotten Deutsche mann!" yelled the lady. "You murderer, you've trapped me! Tomorrow, you'll hang! Help, help!"

"I'll be right down," said Hans.

In a moment he came down carrying a lantern. He looked at Ms. Neuman who stood as if nailed to the earth. At this he started to laugh, hands on his hips.

"Well, well, Ms. Neuman! Ha, Ha, Ha! Good evening to you. Ha, Ha, Ha! I set some traps for skunks and I caught me a lady! What for did the lady come to look in my cellar window? I wrote a warning on the wall for people to stay away. Now you can shout all you want. Let the people come, let them see how the lady prowls around at night looking into the *Deutsche mann*'s window. Oh mein Gott! You can shout for help or stay there until morning. Goodnight to you, Ms. Neuman, goodnight!"

Indeed Ms. Neuman's position was quite awful. If she kept shouting the people would come—what a compromising position to be found in! If she did not shout then she would have to stand all night with her foot in a trap and in the morning to became a sideshow to one and all... And her foot was starting to hurt more and more. Suddenly her head spun around, then stars started swirling and the moon took on the disagreeable face of Mr. Hans Kasche... She fainted.

"Herr Je!" gasped Hans, "If she dies I'll be lynched tomorrow without a trial." The hair on his head stood up from fear.

There was nothing to do but free her. Hans quickly fetched the wrench to open the trap, but this was not easy as Ms. Neuman's robe got in the way. He had to move it a bit and...despite all his fear and distaste for the woman, Hans could not stop himself from casting a glance at the beautiful legs of his enemy. In the moonlight they were white, even marble-like.

One could say that his dislike was turning to pity. He quickly opened the trap, and seeing as the lady had not regained consciousness he picked her up and carried her to her room. On the way he felt the pangs of pity again.

Then he came home and could not shut his eyes for the rest of the night.

Next morning Ms. Neuman did not come out to sing her *Deutsche mann* song at the door of her shop. Perhaps she was ashamed to show her face, or perhaps she was plotting revenge.

It turned out she was plotting revenge. On the evening of that very day the editor of the *Saturday Weekly Review* challenged Hans to a fist fight and blackened his eye at the very start. Hans, however, fought with such fierce desperation, giving his opponent so many hard blows that after an ineffectual defense the editor fell to the ground crying "Enough! Enough!"

By some mysterious agency the entire town was aware of Ms. Neuman's nocturnal adventure. After the fight Hans' pity for his enemy disappeared and again his heart was full of hatred.

Hans had a feeling that a vengeful blow would fall upon him from the hand of an unseen nemesis, and he was soon proven right. Grocery store owners often put up signs at the entrance to their establishments advertising various items for sale. These signs are often headed by the word "Notice" in large black letters. It should also be known that these stores sell ice to the saloons, for no self-respecting American will drink his whiskey or beer without having it chilled down. So it was that Hans suddenly noticed that no one was coming to get ice from him anymore. The large blocks which he had shipped in by rail melted in his cellar. The loss ran into the tens of dollars. Why? How did it happen? Hans could plainly see that even his supporters were hauling blocks of ice from Ms. Neuman's store. He could not figure out how he got in bad with the saloon keepers in town.

He decided to get an explanation. "Why you getting not ice from me?" He asked one of the barkeepers in his broken English, as the man happened to pass by his store.

"Because you haven't got it."

"I not keep ice?"

"Well, how should I know that?"

"Aber, Ich habe ice."

"Well, then what about this?" said the barman, pointing to the sign pasted by the door.

Hans looked at it and went green with anger. On the sign, titled "Notice" someone had purposely scratched out the "t" from the middle of the word. In effect the announcement read "No Ice."

"Donnerwetter!" screamed Hans. Red in the face and shaking from anger he ran into Ms. Neuman's store.

"This is villainy!" he yelled. "Why did you scratch out der letter from mein mittel?"

"I scratched out something from your middle?" she asked pretending not to understand.

"The letter 't', I said! You scratched out my 't'! Aber goddam! I cannot stand this anymore. You will have to pay for the ice! Goddam! Goddam!" He totally lost any remaining composure and stood there shouting like one possessed. Ms. Neuman started to scream. People ran over to see what was the matter.

"Help!" cried Ms. Neuman. "This Deutsche mann has gone mad! He says I scratched him in the middle, what middle? What was I supposed to have scratched out? I scratched nothing. Oh my God, I would scratch out his eyes if I could, nothing more. I, a poor woman, alone... This beast will murder me here!"

And then she started crying. The people around her could not figure out what was going on, but as Americans can't stand a woman's tears, they grabbed Hans and threw him out into the street. He went flying like a projectile right into his own door where he fell full length on the floor.

A week later his store had a beautiful, new, painted sign. On it was a monkey dressed in a striped skirt, a white apron and puffy half-sleeves—just like Ms. Neuman wore. The yellow lettering underneath said "General Store."

The townsfolk came to look at it. Their laughter alerted Ms. Neuman that something was up. She saw the sign and went pale, but did not loose her nerve and immediately shouted: "A store with a monkey, little wonder as Mr. Kasche runs it. Ha!"

But the intended blow struck her right in the heart. Later in the day, she heard the children walking down the street from school. They stopped before the sign shouting: "Oh! That's Miss Neuman! Good Afternoon Miss Neuman!"

This was way too much. In the evening when the *Saturday Weekly Review* editor dropped by she said: "That monkey is supposed to be me. I can't let this pass. He has to take the sign down and remove that offensive ape in front of me."

"What do you intend to do?" he asked.

"I'm going right to the justice of the peace."

"Today?"

"Tomorrow morning."

On the following day she approached Hans and said. "Listen you Deutsche mann! I know the monkey's supposed to be me, but come with me to see the justice of the peace. Let's see what he has to say about this."

"He'll say that I can put up whatever sign I like over my own store."

"We'll see about that," she gasped unable to breathe.

"And how do you know the monkey is supposed to be you?"

"My conscience tells me. Let's go to the justice of the peace, if you don't come the sheriff will drag you over there in chains."

"Alright, I come," said Hans sure of getting his way.

They locked up their respective stores and walked to the justice of the peace while hurling insults at each other. Only at the door to Mr. Dasonville's place did they remember that neither of them knew English well enough to explain the matter. What to do? Of course, get the sheriff who knew both German and English well. So they went for the sheriff.

But the sheriff was in his wagon on the way out. "I'm going to fetch lumber. Good bye!" And he went.

Hans put his hands on his hips. "You will have to wait until tomorrow," he said in his phlegmatic way.

"Me wait! I'd rather die first—or you take down that monkey."

"I will not take monkey down."

"Then you will hang! You'll hang, you Deutsche mann! We can do without the sheriff. The justice of the peace knows what this is about."

"Very well, we do without the sheriff," said Hans.

Unfortunately, Ms. Neuman was wrong. Of all the townspeople, the justice of the peace was the only person unaware of their ongoing quarrel. In his innocence the old man prepared his licorice and lived in the conviction that this was the world's salvation.

He received them in the same way he received everyone—with kindness and grace. "Please stick out your tongues, children, I'll soon write you a prescription…"

Both started to wave their arms to indicate that they had not come for medicine. Ms. Neuman kept repeating, "This is not what we want!"

"So, what is it, then?"

They talked one on top of the other. For every word Hans got in, Ms. Neuman got in ten. Finally, she pointed to her heart to indicate how Hans had hurt her to the quick.

"Oh, yes, I understand now!" said the doctor/justice of the peace.

He opened up a large ledger and started writing. He asked Hans, "How old are you?"

"Thirty-six."

He asked the lady. She could not remember rightly, something around twenty-five.

"Alright. Your full names."

"Hans Kasche"

"Laura Neuman"

"Alright. What do you do?"

They said that they each had a store. Then there were some other questions that neither understood, but answered "yes" just to keep the thing moving.

"Alright." The doctor nodded. The matter was done. He finished writing and then to Laura's great surprise planted a big kiss on her cheek.

She took this as a good omen and went home full of high hopes.

On the way she said to Hans, "That will show you!"

"You can show it to someone else!" answered Hans calmly.

Next morning the sheriff came to visit them. Both parties were at their respective front doors. Hans was smoking his pipe and Ms. Neuman was singing. "Deutsche mann, Deutsche mann, De—Deutsche mann—Deutsche mann, —mann!"

"Do you want to see the justice of the peace?" the sheriff asked.

"We had already been there."

"So, what happened?"

"Mr. Davis, my dear sheriff!" said Ms. Neuman. "Do go there and see what he decided. Soon I'll be at your store for some new shoes. And say to him a word in my favor. After all I am a woman, alone…"

The sheriff went and returned within fifteen minutes. For some unknown reason a crowd of people followed him back.

"Well, so what news?" both inquired.

"All is well, oy, quite well!" said the sheriff.

"And what did the justice of the peace say?"

"What was he to say. He married the two of you."

"Married?!!!"

"It's not uncommon for people to get married."

This was worse than a thunderstroke. Hans and Laura were shaken to the core. Hans' eyes bulged out, he opened his mouth, his tongue hung out and he stared in an idiotic way at Ms. Neuman. Meanwhile, Ms. Neuman's eyes bulged out, her mouth opened and her tongue hung out as she stared at Hans. Both were stunned and stupefied. Then the shouting started.

"I am to be his wife?!"

"I am to be her husband?!"

"Help! Help! I want a divorce—immediately! I don't want this!"

"Neither do I!"

"I'd rather die! Help! I want a divorce! What has happened?"

"My dears," said the sheriff quite affectionately, "why all the noise? The justice of the peace can marry you, but he can't grant a divorce. Why go on so? Are you millionaires from San Francisco to seek a divorce? Do you know what it costs? Oy! Here you are screaming, why? I have some beautiful baby shoes, on sale cheap! Good bye!"

So saying he departed. The townsfolk smiled and went back to their business. The newly married pair was left alone.

"It was that Frenchman," shouted the newly minted wife. "He did this to us because we are Germans."

"Richtig," answered Hans.

"Let's go for the divorce!"

"Me first! It was you who scratched out the 't' from the sign."

"No, no, me first! You were the one who caught me in the trap."

"Lady, I don't want you!"

"Mister, I can't stand you!"

They went their separate ways and locked up their shops. She sat in her room all day, thinking. He sat in his room. The night came, it brought peace. But neither could think about sleeping. Lying in bed each was thinking. He: "Over there is my wife." She: "Over there is my husband." And strange feelings started to stir in their hearts. It was a mixture of hate, anger, pity and loneliness.

Hans started to think about that monkey on the sign over his store. How could he have such a caricature of his wife on display? It seemed to him that he had done a foul thing in having her portrayed in this a way. But this was Ms. Neuman, the woman he hated! She fixed it so that his ice melted unsold. He had caught her in the trap in the moonlight. And then he thought about the shape of the legs that he saw on that night. "Say what you will, there is quite a woman," he thought. "But she can't stand me, and I can't stand her. What a situation! Oh, Herr Gott! He married me, to whom, to Ms. Neuman! And a divorce will cost a pretty sum, even the store will not be enough."

"I am the wife of that, Deutsche mann," thought Ms. Neuman. "I'm not young anymore, or single; but to marry that person! Hans Kasche, the man who caught me in a steel trap. But he did pick me up and he carried me to my room. A very strong man! He lifted me like nothing at all... What's that? Do I hear some noise?"

There was no noise, but Ms. Neuman started to feel fear as she had never felt fear before. "What if he dared to come? Oh, mein Gott!" Then she added in a loud voice, in which there was a strange note of disappointment, "He would not dare... He..."

Her fear got the better of her, "This is how it is for a woman alone..." she continued thinking, "If I had a man it would be safer. I heard about some murders in the vicinity (these were purely imaginary). I don't want to be murdered here. Oh, that Kasche, he has caused all my troubles! Now I have to think about a divorce."

With such thoughts she tossed sleeplessly on her wide American bed and felt very, very lonely. Suddenly she was startled by an actual noise. In the quiet of the night hammering could be plainly heard.

"Jesus! Someone is breaking into my store!" So saying she jumped out of bed and ran to the window, but having had a look she did not calm down immediately. In the light of the moon she could see a ladder and on it the white shape of Hans Kasche banging out the nails that held the store sign in place.

She opened the window quietly. "So, he's decent enough to take it down after all," she thought, and felt as if something was melting in her heart.

Hans pulled out the nails slowly. The sign fell to the ground. He climbed down and knocked the frame apart, then with his calloused hands he rolled the sheet of tin into a scroll and started to put away the ladder.

The lady followed him with her eyes… The night was warm and quiet…

"Hans…" she whispered at him.

"You are not asleep?" he whispered back.

"No! Good Evening to you."

"And a Good Evening to you, too."

"What are you doing?"

"I'm taking down the monkey."

"Thank you, Hans."

A moment of silence.

"Hans…" whispered the female voice again.

"What is it Laura?"

"We have to discuss our divorce."

"Yes, Laura."

"Tomorrow?"

"Tomorrow."

A moment of silence, the moon above was smiling, the dogs were quiet.

"Hans…"

"Yes, Laura?"

"Well, I'm in a hurry to start on the divorce…" Her voice was full of melancholy.

"I'm in a hurry too, Laura!" Hans' voice was sad.

"It's best not to put if off."

"The sooner we discuss it, the better."

"If you would allow me…"

"Then come on up to my room…"

"Let me get properly dressed."

"No need to go through ceremonies…"

The door opened downstairs and then Hans disappeared into the darkness. In a moment he entered a quiet, peaceful and orderly room. Laura had on a white robe and looked beautiful.

"I'm ready to hear you out," said Hans in a soft and subdued voice.

"Well, you see, I would like to go through the divorce but…someone could see us from the street."

"But all the windows are dark…" said Hans.

"So they are," said Laura.

And so began the discussion of the divorce that is not part of this story.

Peace, wonderful peace, returned to Struck Oil City.

NOTES:

According to Sienkiewicz biographer Jozef Szczublewski, Captain Korwin Piotrowski related the core of this story while the author was recuperating at his house in Hayward, California. Piotrowski was a huge, bombastic man with a gift for telling incredible stories in the language of a seventeenth century Polish nobleman. Later, Sienkiewicz would use him as a model for the character of Zagloba in his *Trilogy*. Called "the Polish Falstaff," Zagloba became a cultural icon.

The town of Struck Oil City was probably based on the actual town of Mentryville, California. In 1876, there was an oil strike in the Pico Canyon area, which fueled the creation of a boom town. Sienkiewicz traveled in the vicinity about that time and undoubtedly witnessed the phenomenon. Currently the place is abandoned (partly due to earthquake damage), but is listed on California history rolls.

Sources for the characters are exposed by Marion More Coleman in the *Western Septet* (Cherry Hill Books; Cheshire, CT; 1973). She states in her commentary that persons in the story were taken directly, with only slight modifications, from among the citizens that Sienkiewicz met in Anaheim, California, during his stay there. The town had a German-Jewish constable (Lewis Wartenburg) and a real French physician (Virgil Dassonville). The citizens burned trash in the street and took pot-shots at fowl flying over the town. There was even a drugstore with a fancy glass display window. The merchants in town were Jews and Germans. There was a newspaper, the *Anaheim Gazette*. The author did not have to look far for details to flesh out Piotrowski's lively narration.

THE AUTHORESSES

A HUMOROUS SKETCH ABOUT
CHILDREN, NOT FOR CHILDREN

Marynia and Irka were cousins, they went to school together, and after finishing homework and dinner spent a lot of time playing everyday, and not just on the days when the sun shone. They saw each other even on rainy days, because their homes were on opposite sides of the street. Irka lived with her parents, while Marynia, having been orphaned at three years of age, was in the care of Angela Ocieska, her aunt. Though only twenty-eight, Angela was very pretty and in the sixth year of her widowhood. This young aunt was so very devoted to her charge that no matter how much sympathy she had for a certain young poet, who used the pen-name *Lemiesz* and was the author of a volume of sonnets, she made it quite understood that nothing in the world could make her give up Marynia.

But *Lemiesz*, better known as Mr. Stefan Okinski, made it plainly known that he would never ask for such a separation, because he also loved Marynia with all his heart. The young aunt blushed when he stressed the "also loved" but Mr. Okinski told the truth, for he loved Angela and her adopted child Marynia, and even Irka.

The young ladies, Marynia and Irka, were of the same age, their birthdays being separated only by a few warm

May days. Both were already eleven years old and, of course, were convinced that persons of such age have acquired an excellent knowledge of people and the world, as to be able to act outside strict supervision and use their own judgment. Unfortunately, though eleven is a fairly serious age, adults have the bad habit of ignoring the persons who have attained it, and as a result there are many misunderstandings.

One day Irka came upon such a misunderstanding between Marynia and her aunt.

Initially she did not notice that her friend was rather upset. It could have been due to the fact that Marynia's nose was the only thing visible under her tousled long hair. In addition the windows of the apartment were opened and outside one could see the garden and in it bushes covered in white blossoms, like snow.

"What a wonderful aroma!" Irka called out.

"The jasmine bushes are blooming," answered Marynia in an unsteady voice.

It was then that Irka caught on that something was wrong. "Why are you so upset? What's wrong?"

"How can I not be upset, when it's always the same old thing?"

"What's the same old thing?'

"The fact that my auntie still treats me like a child."

"And you think that my mother and father don't?"

Marynia straightened her hair and started to explain while gesticulating. "I'm in the twelfth year of my life and I'm being looked after like a five year old baby. This is really difficult to endure. My auntie does not seem to know that I know just about everything and the things I don't, I can figure out."

Irka came quickly, throwing her braid back. She was suddenly very much interested and engaged. "You figured something out? What was it?"

"Various things," answered Marynia. "Don't you?"

"Naturally. But to be absolutely sure..."

"Well, no, not to be absolutely sure. In any case I know enough that I can read everything, but sometimes auntie wants me to read stories only intended for children."

"Definitely, one cannot accept such a situation," stated Marynia with dignity.

Then she added, "Did you get a talking-to for reading something?"

"And how! An hour ago in the cabinet I found what seemed a very interesting and absorbing book entitled *The Natural Son* and started reading it. By the time I finished the first few pages auntie came in and took it away. Then she lectured me about reading things not intended for young ladies."

"How awful! A natural son... It must have been very interesting! But what is a 'natural' son?"

"Well, a natural son is one...that well...I can't say precisely but as far as I can figure out that if there is a natural son then there may be an artificial one."

"And what do you mean by artificial?"

Marynia's brows arched onto her forehead. Not only her face, but her posture indicated the effects of mental exertion. "An artificial one is one that...that..."

"You don't know, but you said you figured it all out?"

"Wait. This is what I figured out. A natural son is one that is born after the wedding, and an artificial one is born before the wedding."

"Could be. Could be. In such case the two of us could only have artificial sons."

"Probably."

"Oh, that would be quite something!"

This kind of event appeared to be quite amusing to Irka, because she burst out with laughter. Then she asked. "Tell me, would you like to have an artificial son?"

But Marynia raised her sky blue eyes as befitting a serious person who does not express a wish or desire without giving it some forethought. She said, "I'd rather have a fox-terrier." In a moment she added. "White, with one black ear, and a black spot on his back."

"I'd rather have a pair."

"True, that would be much more fun." Then she sighed and, like a woman used to disappointments, stated melancholically, "This will probably never happen to us."

Suddenly, Irka was plunged into doubt. "Listen Marynia, what if I figured it out wrong—what if an artificial son is merely a doll?"

"Then some other girl can have it. I'm too old to be playing with dolls."

"Especially when people are around."

"Especially when people are around. I understand precisely."

"In the end, we don't know anything."

"If only auntie would let me read *The Natural Son*, then I would figure out about the artificial one, of course... A woman, no matter how old, is not able to figure out everything."

"So, sneak the book out of the cabinet and read it!"

In Marynia's little heart there lived a person of conscience and integrity, so she splayed out her hands and said, "I gave my word that I won't take any books from the cabinet without auntie's knowledge."

"If you gave your word, that's another matter," said Irka who was no less honest than her friend.

Silence fell for a moment.

"That's a shame about auntie," said Marynia, "if she was not so good to me, I would probably grow to hate her."

"But you can't possibly hate auntie Angela."

"When I had the chicken pox she sat by my bedside until I was better. She's not only pretty but so wonderful in many other things."

"Like my dad."

"But we are grown and it should not be that people keep things from us, like rationing candy to children so they would not get a bellyache from having too much."

"It is a sorry situation, and inappropriate."

"But there is no way to get around it."

Then Irka, who was more proactive and inventive than Marynia, started to walk up and down the room and shake her dark head. Finally, she jumped on the couch and bounced on the cushions. She started repeating, "There's a way! There's a way!"

"How?" asked Marynia.

"This will surely work!"

"Tell me…now!"

"We will write a novel."

"A novel?"

"Yes, one that is horribly indecent and then we'll send it to a publisher by messenger. You remember, Mr. Okinski was telling auntie Angela that the newspapers were looking for long and short stories to publish. So, whatever we send will get published right away, especially if the people at the publishing office don't know that we are not quite grown up."

Now even the serious minded Marynia started bouncing up and down. "That is brilliant! We'll write a novel."

"A huge romance, a love story."

"A gentleman in love with a lady…"

"Yes!"

At that moment Marynia stopped jumping up and down. "But," she asked, "what does that have to do with reading other books?"

"Don't you get it? Once our novel is published in the press, your auntie and my parents will say that this story is not for us and won't allow us to read it. Then we'll go and prove to them that we are the authoresses."

"Great! Oh, this will be ever so much fun! Then, of course they'll have to let us read everything!"

The future authoresses grabbed each other's arms and started to whirl around. But because stable minds cannot indulge in idle play—especially when it makes them dizzy—they stopped. Then Irka said, "Let's not lose time. We'll start right now…"

"Let's write," Marynia agreed.

In a flash they sat down at the table where Marynia usually did her homework. There was ink, pens, and paper at the ready. It was only necessary to call on inspiration and get started.

Why is it that inspiration tends to hover just under the ceiling, is a difficult question. But it is surely so, for though no one told Irka and Marynia about it, they started to look at the ceiling.

For an extended time there was silence at the table. Meanwhile, underneath, little legs clad in black stockings and yellow shoes dangled back and forth in an uninterrupted rhythm. Strictly speaking, it may not have been very serious, but natural for persons whose legs were not quite yet long enough to reach the floor.

Marynia was first to interrupt the silence and the leg swinging.

"Can two people write a novel?"

"Of course," said Irka. "Mr. Okinski was talking to my parents about this very thing, when he read to them about a novel written by two Frenchmen. If two Frenchmen can write together, so can we."

"So one will recite, and the other write?"

"No. We will compose together, and each will write on her own sheet of paper. Then we will take our papers and think about it some more. If any new ideas come then we'll consult about it tomorrow."

"Good. Let's get started."

The leg swinging under the table started again, but did not last long.

"What will we name our hero?" asked Irka.

"Whom?"

"Don't you understand. The gentleman who loves the lady…"

"Of course I understand. Let's name him Stefan."

"And the woman will be Angela, like auntie?"

"But no… We better find other names. Auntie would get mad at me thinking that we were writing about her and Mr. Okinski. I'll tell you a secret. I heard the servants talking that Mr. Okinski wants to marry auntie. Then I asked her to see if it was true, but she only got red in the face and told me to keep quiet."

"I heard something too. Dad told mother that 'Stefan's ready anytime, but she's not quite there.' I was very interested in finding out what that meant, but they told me to keep my nose in my own business."

"So we can't use Stefan and Angela?"

"No, so what will be their names?"

"He could be named Julius."

"Great. A fine name. And she?"

"Idalia."

"Wonderful. Apparently you do have talent."

"Perhaps I do have some," admitted Marynia modestly. The pens had not yet started to make marks on paper. Their other ends instead found themselves being chewed on by the two writers. This was accompanied by looks up and down and other signs indicating a lack of confidence.

Suddenly Marynia put down her pen. "But what will happen if they do let us read our own story?"

"There's a method for this."

"Do tell."

"I told you that the story must be terribly indecent, absolutely shocking, horrible."

"Oh yes, true!"

"Then my parents and auntie Angela will know that there's nothing they can keep from us!"

After a moment of concentration Irka's face started to brighten, probably from the influence of an ingenious idea.

"Let's start this way: 'Julius and Idalia, as soon as they met at a ball, started to behave in a most indecent way...'"

"Excellent!" said Marynia. "They will definitely not let us read that."

The pens started to scratch in earnest, but after such a promising start Marynia broke off. "You, see...fine... First they had to meet, talk with each other, and fall in love. I am absolutely sure that in stories not intended for children they always fall in love."

"Oh, I am sure of that. So we'll make it like this, 'Julius and Idalia first met at a ball, then they talked, then fell in love, and started to behave in a very indecent way...'"

"That is better, but let's think about these indecent things they are going to do."

"Let's...have them kiss."

"Well, is that enough? Mr. Okinski kisses me on the head, and he kisses auntie Angela on the hand—and always three times."

"But what if Julius kisses Idalia on the lips?"

"At the ball? That would be very indecent. What else?"

"What do you mean, 'What else?'"

"Because what we've got runs about three sentences—maybe five. But a novel is a whole book."

"Right. Let's think up some more indecent things for them to do."

Inspiration, hovering just under the ceiling turned out to be absolutely impermeable to entreaties from the desperate looks of the authoresses. Silence reigned in the room.

"They could then hug each other," said Marynia.

"No! When people kiss they don't put their hands behind their backs, but hold each other. It all happens in the course of things."

"Yes," Marysia admitted, "we must think up something that happens after all the hugging and kissing." Then she thought deeply and raised her eyes, interjecting timidly. "What if they stole the cake that was prepared for all the guests?"

"Foo!" answered Irka, "Like little kids! That would be gluttony, not love."

"You are quite right. It is necessary that they commit some indecency out of love."

"But what?"

Marynia sighed, "It's not at all easy to write a novel."

"But writers somehow manage."

Marynia came up with a different idea. "What if we ask Mr. Okinski? When he comes to call, auntie always takes her time in fixing her hair before she sees him. That would be a good time to pose the question. I won't tell him we are writing a novel, but I'll just ask what happens in love after the kissing and hugging."

Irka rubbed her forehead. "I'm totally at a loss as to what one can do after that. But Mr. Okinski is not a novelist but a poet. Do you think poets know what goes on? Do you think he would guess what we are doing? But wait…I know!"

"What? What?"

"We will write like this: 'Julius and Idalia first met at the ball, then fell in love, behaved indecently, and then he seduced her.'"

"What does that mean?"

"I'm not quite sure, but I can tell you how I heard the word. Daddy was reading some story to mom and I was in the adjoining room. I distinctly heard this sentence 'After that unfortunate day when Edward seduced Magdalena…' Then mom interrupted his reading and said 'Careful, Irka is near.' Then daddy asked me to go to another room. From this I concluded it is something they don't want us to know about."

"But I think that *se-duce* must mean to take away, from Latin *se*—away and *duce*—to lead."

"I think it must be something worse than that."

"But you know that after a wedding the couples almost always take a trip abroad. That means he takes her away. It's a custom."

"So the worst thing we can write is: 'Julius and Idalia, after meeting and falling in love and various indecencies, married and then he seduced her.'"

"But if it's a custom there's nothing so indecent about it."

"So why did my mother say, 'Careful, Irka is near.'?"

"Yes, that is strange and we should think about it."

After this incisive comment there was an extended moment of thought where the authoresses were confronted by the fact that in writing a novel there are all kinds of unforeseen difficulties.

"Oh!, if only some one would want to seduce one of us!"

"At least we would know what it's all about," added Marynia.

Any further conversation was preempted by the doorbell and the arrival at the door of Mr. Stefan Okinski, also known as *Lemiesz*. Even as *Lemiesz*, the author of three dozen sonnets, he still resembled a very nice man. He did not have a depressing gaze, he washed every morning, wore a jacket and not a cape, his hair was well barbered. This was all good evidence that he was not trying to prop up his talent with a cape or long hair. Since he was the inheritor of an estate that was much greater than his talent, then no one envied him the sonnets and he was well received and even admired by women. Arriving, he held out a bouquet of flowers and a box tied with a pink ribbon. On entering he greeted the little authoresses in a familiar way, kissing their foreheads.

"Please have a seat," said Marynia, "Such beautiful flowers." And then she looked at the box.

"The flowers are for your aunt, the box of chocolates is for you two," he said. "Is your aunt here?"

"Yes. She must have heard the bell, but she will take a moment. When you come she always fixes her hair, changes her bow or even powders her face so she won't blush."

Mr. Okinski put the box on the table, then took both of Marynia's hands into his own and clasping them tightly he stated with enthusiasm on his face, "You, my little cherub, you should know how I enjoyed hearing that, and I do love you for it."

Marynia first freed her little hands, lowered her head and looked adoringly at Mr. Okinski. She twisted her braided pigtail as she asked, "Do you really love me?"

"Like I love few people in the world."

"And you will give me an honest answer to a question?"

"With the greatest of assurances."

"Well," started Marynia timidly, "this could be a little improper, but it's important to me and Irka."

"So? So?"

"Well, you see Irka and me would like to know what it is when a gentleman seduces a lady?"

Anyone who would, at that moment, be called upon to deduce Mr. Okinski's intelligence from the expression on his face would have never suspected that he was the author of three dozen sonnets—or even three sonnets. At that instant the unhappy poet showed a face so surprised and even idiotic, that one would be hard pressed to find a similar one in all of Parnassus.

"God have mercy! Marynia… What are you…"

So Marynia, thinking that he did not understand her, repeated the question in a different form. "I'd like to know if the seduction takes place before the wedding or after, and what's it all about?"

"Marynia!!!" called out Okinski in desperation. And the expression on his face was not even idiotic but completely befuddled.

"You have to tell me," Marynia insisted, "you promised!"

"Quiet! I have no intention of telling you!"

"Then you probably don't know yourself!"

Then Irka pouted her lips in disdain. "I said that poets don't know about these things."

"Obviously," added Marynia, "but all the novelists do!"

"Obviously!"

With their indignation against poets bordering on contempt, the two authoresses directed their disdain at Mr. Okinski. Meanwhile, the auntie entered. Marynia ran to her and under the influence of grave disappointment and great disillusion called out, "Auntie, auntie, you should never marry Mr. Okinski, he doesn't even know what seduction is!"

This caused an even greater disaster, because the auntie was taken aback even more than the poet was, and she decided that in such situations the only way out for a woman was to faint! She collapsed heavily onto the couch, closed her eyes and remained motionless.

The room filled with panic. Mr. Okinski ran to help shouting "Water, water!" in a voice so wild that it could indicate the house had caught on fire. Marynia and Irka ran for the carafe. The auntie lay there, eyes closed, with Mr. Okinski sitting by her. He put his arms around her, leaned her head against his chest and started to talk in a manner that was altogether sensitive, fearful and pathetic, "Awake my angel! Awake my angel!"

Meanwhile, his moustache migrated closer and closer toward the auntie's face.

* * * *

How it all ended and whether the angel awoke is not part of this story.

Readers, however, should be informed that the romance novel *Julius and Idalia* never saw the light of day and the young authoresses, to literature's great loss, decided to put off their writing efforts for an extended period of time.

THE THIRD ONE

WARSAW - 1889

I

The rent on the studio in which Swiatecki and I lived and painted was unpaid. First, because between the two of us we had exactly five rubles; and second, we had a true revulsion toward the paying of rent.

We painters are often called squanderers, but I would be the first to buy vodka rather than to waste money by giving it to the landlord.

As for the landlord, he was not a bad man at heart, and we soon found a "cure" for him. When, usually in the morning, he came to collect, Swiatecki, who slept on a straw mattress spread on the floor and used, as a coverlet, a Turkish curtain, which doubled as a background for portraits, would sit up and cry out in an eerie voice.

"Good to see you sir, for I dreamed that you were dead!"

The landlord, who was superstitious and obviously afraid of death, would become extraordinarily confused. Swiatecki would then stretch out on the mattress, fold his hands across his chest and continue.

"I saw you just like this. You were wearing oversized gloves and patent leather shoes. In reality you were not unlike yourself."

I would then add, "Sometimes these dreams don't come true…"

I think it was the "sometimes" that threw the landlord into a state of panic. Finally, enraged, he would exit slamming the door. We would hear him going down the steps—four at a time. All the while he cursed all that the world holds sacred. Fortunately he was kind enough not to send for the sheriff.

True, we could not be dispossessed of much. He probably figured that the studio would be rented by artists anyway and he would get the same or worse.

Unfortunately, the keen edge of our "method" dulled with time. The landlord gradually became accustomed to the idea of death. Therefore, Swiatecki decided to do a series of three painting: *Expiration*, *Interment*, and *Awaking from a Coma*. In all three the central figure was to be our landlord.

Such grave subjects are Swiatecki's specialty. He, according to his own admission, paints "stiffs." Perhaps that is why no one wants to buy his paintings, even though he has talent. He sent two of his "stiffs" to the Paris Salon Exhibition. I sent my *Jews by the Vistula,* which was promptly rechristened *Jews by the Rivers of Babylon* in the official catalogue. We anxiously awaited the decision of the contest jury.

Swiatecki, of course, predicted that all would go in the worst possible way. He maintained that the jury was composed of idiots, and if they were not idiots, then I am an idiot, our paintings are idiotic, and awarding us any kind of prize would be the height of idiocy.

I cannot begin to describe how much of my blood that ape has fouled during the two years we had lived together.

Anthony Swiatecki's entire ambition is to pass for a *moral stiff*. He also pretends to be a drunkard, something he isn't. He downs two or three shots of vodka while looking about to check if we are watching him. If he is not sure he will elbow someone and looking him askew in the face ask, "Look how low I've fallen…eh?"

We tell him that he is a moron, and this upsets him greatly. Nothing puts him in a worse mood than disbelief in his moral downfall. By and by though, he is a stout fellow, ready to come through in a pinch.

Once we were lost in the mountains somewhere near Zell-am-See. Night had caught us and it was easy to break one's neck in the dark.

He said to me, "Listen Wladek, you have more talent—it would be a shame to lose you. I'll go first and if I fall, wait it out until dawn, then go and find your way."

"You will not," I said. "I'll go first, my eyes are better!"

To this Swiatecki replied, "If I don't finish here, I'll wind up in the gutter…it's all the same."

We began to argue.

Meanwhile, it got darker than inside a cow's belly. At last we agreed to go and meet our fate together. Swiatecki picked up his bundle and went first.

We were walking along a ridge. At first it was fairly wide but then it started to narrow. As far as we could tell there were bottomless depths on either side. The path got narrower, fragments of rock began to slide out from under our feet…

"On all fours," said Swiatecki, "no other way."

In truth, there was no other way, so we proceeded forward like two primates.

Soon, however, even this was inadequate, as the width of the ridge got to be no greater than that of a horse's back. Swiatecki mounted it, and I after him. We moved by pushing hand over hand along the ridge all the while inflicting the most extraordinary damage to our clothes.

After a time I heard Swiatecki's voice.

"Wladek!"

"What?"

"This is it—the end!"

"Well?"

"Nothing, this must be the edge of a cliff!"

"Take a rock and throw it, we may be able to judge the depth!"

In the darkness I could hear him groping for a chunk of weathered rock. Then he spoke.

"Here goes! Listen."

We were all ears.

Silence.

"Did you hear anything?"

"No."

"A fine fix, it must be a couple hundred feet!"

"Throw again."

He found a larger fragment and heaved it.

No sound.

"What the devil, no bottom, or what?" cussed Swiatecki.

"We will have to wait until dawn, there is nothing else we can do."

So we sat. Swiatecki threw more rocks with no luck. An hour passed, then another. Then I heard Swiatecki's voice.

"Wladek, don't fall asleep…have you got a cigarette?"

It was discovered that while I did have cigarettes, we were both out of matches. Despair! By then it was probably one in the morning, if that.

A light drizzle began to come down. All around the darkness was impenetrable. I came to the conclusion that living in cities, among people, we have no real idea what silence it. The silence about us was so intense that my ears were ringing. I could almost hear the blood pounding in my veins—my heartbeat was like a drumbeat. At first I found the situation interesting.

Sitting at the edge of a cliff in the dead of night is not an adventure for common sots. Unfortunately, the cold started to get to me and, worse luck, Swiatecki started to philosophize.

"What is life? Life is filth! They say *art*, *art*. To hell with it and me, It's all an aping of nature, and ugly too. Twice, I saw the Paris Salon. There were so many painting the canvas would suffice to make mattresses for all the Jews in the world. And for what? The worst kowtowing to the tastes of merchants and bourgeois. All calculated for quick sale and filling the belly. The very lack of art—nothing less. If there was such a thing as a muse of painting she probably would get struck with paralysis at such a sight. Fortunately, art does not exist, only nature. But nature is filth anyway, better to end it all, once and for all. I'd do it if I had some vodka, but as I don't, I'll live. I swore that I would not die sober."

I was used to Swiatecki's babbling, but under the circumstances it put me in a somber mood. Finally, he emptied himself and shut up. He threw a few more rocks, repeated "No sound" and then silence descended for three hours.

Hearing cawing and the flutter of wings, I thought that dawn would break soon. It was still dark, yet I was certain that hawks and eagles were beginning to circle above the chasm. The sounds tore the darkness above us. The voices were so numerous that I imagined entire legions of eagles flying above us. I was glad for it, as they signaled the coming day.

After a while, I saw my own hands leaning on the rock, then a silhouette of Swiatecki's shoulders against a lighter background. This background grew lighter by the minute. A pleasing silver-gray light began to reflect off the rock, then off Swiatecki's shoulders and fill the darkness just as if someone had poured a sliver fluid into the blackness. This fluid, in mixing became gray, then pearl. There was a certain rawness and dampness not only on the rock, but even the air felt moist.

Dawn broke moment by moment.

I observed the changes in coloration and tried to remember them, painting a little in my soul. Just then I was interrupted by Swiatecki's screams.

"Phooey! Idiots!"

Then his back disappeared from sight!

"Swiatecki," I hollered, "what are you doing?"

"Don't scream! Look!"

I looked over and what did I see? Here we were on a rock outcrop that descended into a pasture which was just two feet below. The thick moss covering the pasture deadened the sound of the rocks we threw. Across the level ground, in the distance, I could see a road. Above were crows which I mistook for eagles. All we had to do was to let our legs down and walk peacefully to our lodge.

Instead we sat on that outcrop, teeth chattering, the whole blessed night.

I do not know why now, while we were both awaiting the landlord's monthly visit, I had thought of this adventure which took place over a year and a half ago. It was so clear in my mind that it might have happened yesterday.

All this gave me a strange new hope. "Remember, Tony, when we thought we were sitting at the edge of a precipice, but it turned out to be a smooth road? It could be like that now. Here we are, poorer than a couple church mice, the landlord would like to throw us into the street, but this could change. Suddenly a door to fame and fortune could swing open and…"

Swiatecki was just then sitting on the edge of his mattress pulling on his boots. All the while he muttered how life is composed of putting shoes on in the morning and taking them off at night, and that only he has brains who has courage to hang himself. He, Swiatecki, has not done so yet only because he is a total idiot and a craven coward besides.

My outburst of optimism interrupted his ruminations. He lifted up his fish-like eyes and said, "You have a lot to be happy about. A few days ago Slusowski booted you out of his house and his daughter's heart. Today the landlord will kick you out of the studio."

Unfortunately, that was the truth.

Three days ago, I was the fiancé of Kathy Slusowski. On Tuesday, yes just last Tuesday, I received the following letter from her father.

Dear Sir!
Our daughter, acceding to the persuasions of her parents has agreed to end a relationship which would mean nothing but unhappiness for her. She could always find

shelter in her mother's arms and under her father's roof, but it was up to us, the parents to prevent such a finality. Not only your material position but your thoughtless character, which even with careful effort, you were not able to conceal, force our daughter to break off her relations with you. This, however, will not affect our kindly regard toward you.

    With respect,

     Heliodor Slusowski,

     Undersecretary of the Treasury

Thus sounded the letter.

I would more or less agree that my "financial position" could not provide a dog with shoes, but as to what that pathetic gorilla would want from my character, I truly can't comprehend.

Kathy's head recalls a silhouette from the romantic period, and it would be nice if she wore her hair that way. I even went as far as to ask her to change to that fashion, but it was all for naught, as she does not understand these things.

The coloration of her face is so warm and pleasant, as if painted on by Fortuni.

I loved her honestly and from the day I received Slusowski's letter I behaved as if I had been poisoned. Finally, on the second day I did feel better. At last I decided—"If it's not meant to be, it's not."

The thing that helped to ease the blow was thinking about the Salon exhibition and my *Jews*. I was sure that the painting was good. Swiatecki, of course, prophesied that it wouldn't be permitted even in the foyer of the Salon.

I started painting it a year ago. This is the way it came about.

I was taking an evening stroll by the Vistula. I look, an apple vendor's cart had turned over. The street urchins are fishing apples out of the water, while on the bank sits a Jewish family. They are in such despair that they are not even crying. Their hands are folded in an expression of grief. Their eyes are staring into the water as if transfixed. There is an old Jew, a beggar patriarch; an old Jewish woman; a young man, a colossal Maccabean type; a young girl, freckled somewhat but with tremendous character of nose and lips; and two Jewish kids.

The sun is setting. The woods on the river have taken on a glow. Farther down where the river has overflowed the banks there are red, ultramarine, steel, purple and violet tones playing on the water. The perspective is infinite—paradise! The blending of colors is so superb that the soul wants to scream with joy. All about is quiet, light, peaceful. Melancholy hangs over it all—one could just cry—and there in the midst of it all is the group portraying such sorrow as if they had posed in studios from infancy.

Then and there it hit me. That is my painting.

Fortunately, I had my inseparable pad and charcoal with me, so I started to sketch. To the Jews I yelled, "Stay right there, don't move. A ruble to each of you—until dusk."

My Jews quickly caught on and froze into the ground. I kept sketching. The urchins came up from the water and started to shout vulgar insults at me—about painters in general. But I answered in their own tongue and immediately befriended them. They even stopped chucking wood chips at the Jews, as not to spoil my work.

After that the group's humor improved remarkably. "Jews," I shout, "be sad!" To which the old woman answered, "Kind sir, but why should we be sad if you promised us a ruble each? Let him be sad who has no income!"

I had to threaten not to pay them.

For two evenings I sketched the group. Later they posed in the studio. Let Swiatecki say what he will, the painting is good. It portrays the honest truth and a lot of nature. The faces might have been prettier, but they could not have been more real or had more character.

Remembering all this helped to soften the loss of Kathy. When Swiatecki recalled my broken engagement it seemed ages ago. By that time he was working on the other boot, so I lighted the samovar.

Old Mrs. Antoniowa dropped in with our morning rolls. Swiatecki has been trying to talk her into hanging herself for some time now. Finally we sat down to breakfast.

"What the hell are you so happy about?" asks Swiatecki.

"Oh, I don't really know. Just wait, something unusual will happen to us!"

In the same moment we heard the sound of feet on the steps leading up to the studio.

"The landlord! Some surprise!" says Swiatecki.

In the same instant he gulps down his tea, which is so hot that it makes tears pop into his eyes. He then leaps out of the kitchen and attempts to hide behind a rack of costumes in the studio.

From his hiding place he gasps, "You talk to him, he likes you!"

"He's absolutely wild about you!" I answer dashing for the rack. "You talk to him."

Then the door opens and in comes…not the landlord, but the concierge of the house inhabited by the Slusowski family.

We fall out from among the costumes.

"I have a letter for you," he says.

I take it. Holy Moses! It's from Kathy! I tear into the envelope and read the contents.

> I am quite sure of my parents' forgiveness. Come at once without regard for the early hour. We have just returned from taking the waters in the park. K.

I am not quite sure what the parents are going to forgive me for, exactly. Unfortunately, I have no time to think as my head is swimming from sheer amazement.

After a while, I hand the letter to Swiatecki and turn to the messenger.

"Friend, tell the lady I'm coming. Wait! I don't have change, but here is a three ruble note. Get change, keep one, and bring back the rest."

Speaking aside, I never saw him again. He knew, the little vermin, that I would not cause trouble in the Slusowski household and used his position shamelessly. Unfortunately, at the time I did not even take notice of it.

"Well?" I ask Swiatecki.

"Nothing, every calf will find a butcher."

The hurry in which I dressed did not permit me to think of a fitting insult to hurl at Swiatecki.

II

A quarter of an hour later I ring the bell at the Slusowskis.

Kathy opens the door herself. She is beautiful. With her is the warmth of dreams and in the folds of her blue dress, the freshness of the morning right from the park. Her hat, which she has removed, has ruffled her hair. Her face is smiling, her eyes are smiling, her moist lips are smiling. She is like the morning itself. I take her hand and kiss it.

She leans over and asks, "Who loves better?"

Then, taking my hand, she leads me before the parents. Old Slusowski bears the expression of a Roman who is sacrificing his only child *pro patria*. The mother is crying into her coffee, as they are seated at the breakfast table. At our appearance they rise.

Papa Slusowski decrees, "Reason and duty would have me say 'No!' but a parent's heart has laws of its own. If this is weakness, may God try me for it."

Here he lifts his gaze as if to answer should the heavenly tribunal decide to open the case. I have never seen anything so Roman except perhaps the salami and macaroni sold in the Italian quarter. The moment is so weighty that a hippopotamus would burst from emotion. This is further heightened when Mrs. Slusowski, with outstretched arms and tears in her eyes, proclaims, "My children! If the world is ever cruel to you, you may always find shelter here!…here!"

I'm no dummy! I'm not ever taking shelter there… there! If Kathy made me the same offer, that would be another thing. Even with all the theatrics I am impressed with their kindness, and my heart brims with gratitude.

I am so shaken that I begin consuming alarming quantities of coffee, so much so that old Slusowski begins to eye the supplies. Kathy just keeps on pouring, while I try to give her little knee a squeeze under the table. She just backs off, shaking her head and smiling so impishly that I nearly jump out of my skin.

I spend an hour and a half there, but must run as a pupil awaits me at the studio. I give lessons and collect some notes with the government seal on them; these I often lose.

Kathy and her mother lead me to the door, which only infuriates me for I wanted Kathy alone to show me out. The lips on that girl...

My walk back takes me through the park. Many people are returning from taking the waters. While en route I notice that people are stopping to look at me. I hear my name being whispered. Young ladies dressed in all shades of percale are giving looks, as if to say "Welcome, stranger!" What the devil, am I famous or what?

I walk on, more of the same. At the door I collide with the landlord, just like a ship on a rock. Oh! The rent!

But he approaches me and says, "Good Sir! I know I am a bother sometimes, but believe me, I have so much... oh, allow me please!"

So saying he embraces me. Oh, I see, Swiatecki must have told him that I will be getting married. He must think that now the rent will be paid on a regular basis. Let him think that.

I thunder upstairs. On the way I hear noise issuing from our quarters. The interior is dim from cigarette smoke. There's Jules Rzysinski, Frank Cepkowski, old Sludecki and others. All are having a wonderful time passing my pupil around in the smoke above their heads. Seeing me, they release him, barely alive, in the center of the studio.

Then they produce an inhuman tumult, "Congratulations, congratulations!"

"Up with him!"

In a flash I'm up in the air, and for a while they amuse themselves by tossing me up and down all the while howling like a pack of wild wolves. When, finally, I get to the ground I announce that they are all invited to the wedding, especially Swiatecki whom I am reserving for best man.

At this Swiatecki raises his hands and speaks.

"This dimwit thinks that we are congratulating him on his upcoming marriage!"

"Well, what else would you be congratulating me on?"

"What, don't you know?" I hear from all directions.

"I don't know what in the blazes you are talking about!"

"Give him a copy of the morning *Flyer*, the morning *Flyer*!" yells Wach Protekiewicz.

A copy of the *Flyer* is thrust into my hands as they continue shouting, "Look in the correspondence!"

I look at the correspondence section and read the following:

> From the Flyer's own correspondent in Paris. Magorski's painting "Jews by the Rivers of Babylon" received the great gold medal in this year's Salon. The critics cannot find words enough to describe the artist's genius. Albert Wolff calls the painting "a revelation." Baron Hirsh offers 15,000 franks.

I feel weak! Help! I'm so stupefied that I cannot utter a word. I knew the painting turned out well, but I had no inkling of such a success.

The copy of the *Flyer* falls from my hands. My friends pick it up and continue to read.

> Item one— We hear from the artist's own lips that he intends to exhibit the painting in our fair city.
>
> Item two— To the question posed by the president of the Art Institute as to whether the work would be shown in Warsaw the artist replied, "I would rather not sell it

in Paris than not show it in Warsaw." We trust that the above will be read by our progeny (as far in the future as God will allow) on the artist's tombstone.

Item three— After reading the announcement of his success, the artist's mother suffered a severe emotional shock.

Item four— At the time of this printing we are informed that the artist's mother is feeling better.

Item five— The artist has received invitations to exhibit his work in all the capitals of Europe.

I recover under the force of these boldfaced lies. Ostrzynski, the editor of the *Flyer* and ex-rival for Kathy's hand, must have gone berserk. This surpasses all measure. Of course I will exhibit the painting in Warsaw, but for one—I spoke to no one about the matter, two—the president of the Art Institute did not speak to me, three—I told the president of the Art Institute nothing, four—my mother has been dead for nine years, and five—no one invited me to do anything.

What if, I begin to think, the correspondence is a genuine as the news items. Good grief!

Over six months ago Ostrzynski, my rival for Kathy's hand, got his walking papers even though the parents favored him. He could be trying to make a fool of me. If that is the case he will "pay with his head or some such thing" as goes the libretto of a currently fashionable operetta.

My friends, however, try to convince me that even though the news items are phoney, the correspondence must be real.

At that time Stach Kosowicz arrives with a copy of the *Pole*. The correspondence is in it as well. I relax and begin breathing again.

The congratulations begin in earnest.

Old Sludecki, false through and through but sweet as syrup, shakes my hand and says, "Good God! I always knew you had talent! I always stood up for you (he called me an ass)…but perhaps you would not wish that such a *fa-presto* would call you *friend*, but then forgive an old habit, good God…"

Deep in my heart I hope he hangs, but I can't give him an answer for in that moment Karminski pulls me aside. He whispers as if not to be overheard.

"Perhaps you need some money, my friend, if so just give the word."

Karminski is well known among us for his selflessness. Now and again he will say to one of us, "If you need money my friend…" and then just try to find him. In reality he has money. I answer that if I can't find it elsewhere, I will go to him.

Others come up, fellows good as gold, and hug me until my poor sides ache. Finally Swiatecki comes up, I can see he is touched but is trying to conceal it.

"I see you will turn Jew," he says brusquely, "but congratulations anyway."

"I see you will turn idiot, but thanks anyway," I answer. We embrace.

Wach Protokiewicz mentions something about his throat being dry. I'm broke, but Swiatecki has two rubles, other have some money too. After the collection—punch!

They drink my health, toss me into the air again and when I tell them that the matter with Kathy is all fixed up they drink to her health.

Then Swiatecki corrals me and says, "Don't you think, you gullible moron, that they did not read the paper before the young lady wrote to you?"

Damnation! I have the sensation of being clubbed repeatedly. One side of the horizon gets lighter, while on the other it is devilishly dark. I'm not surprised at the Slusowskis but that Kathy should be capable of such cold blooded calculation!

It is quite probable that they saw the story while in the park taking the waters. After that they called me.

At first, I want to run to the Slusowski house and have it out. Unfortunately, I cannot leave my guests.

In addition Ostrzynski arrives on the scene. He is elegant, cold, self-assured, gloved—as always. Cleverness surrounds him like an aura, for here is a wit shod on all fours.

From the door he begins to wave his cane protagonistically. "Congratulations, maestro, my congratulations!"

He stresses the "my" as if his congratulations were worth more than anyone else's.

It just may be so.

"Where on earth did you find such lies!" I shout. "As you see me here, I have just learned everything from your paper!"

"Why should I worry about that?" answers Ostrzynski flatly.

"But I spoke to no one about exhibiting the painting!"

"Well, now you are doing it," he adds phlegmatically.

"But he's got no mother and she didn't go weak!" adds Wojtek Michalak.

"I am not concerned with these details," answers Ostrzynski as he removes his other glove.

"Is the correspondence real?"

"Yes."

This assurance calms me. From sheer gratitude I pour him a glass of punch. He puts the glass to his lips and says, "Here's to your health, and a second toast to… double congratulations!" Then he shrugs his shoulders.

"How did you know?"

"Old Slusowski was at my office before eight this morning."

Swiatecki begins to mutter something about people being rotten in general. I just can't take it anymore, and grab for my hat. Ostrzynski exits with me, but I quickly outdistance him. In a few minutes I ring the bell at the Slusowski residence.

Kathy answers, the parents are not at home.

"Kathy," I address her harshly, "did you know about the correspondence?"

"Yes, I knew." She is quite calm.

"Oh, Kathy!"

"What else could I do, dear. Don't be surprised at my parents, they had to have some sensible reason to give consent."

"But you, Kathy?"

"I just took advantage of the opportunity. Can you fault me for that, Wladek?"

Suddenly, everything seems clear and I admit that Kathy makes sense. Strictly speaking, why did I run over there like a madman?

Meanwhile, Kathy puts her head on my shoulder, I take her about the waist. She then leans her head back, closes her eyes and presents her little red mouth whispering, "No, no, Wladek, not now, after the wedding, please."

In spite of her plea, I press my lips against hers and we remain in this position as long as the process of res-piration allows. Kathy's eyes are swimming. She covers them to utter, "And I asked you not to…"

That phrase and the look she gives me move me to kiss her again. When you love a girl, you naturally have a greater desire to kiss, rather than, for example, to beat her.

And I love Kathy without measure or reason. In life, until death, after death! Her or none—that is it!

In a tired voice Kathy expresses the fear that I will lose respect for her. Dearest creature, where on earth does she get such ideas! I calm her down and we begin to talk sensibly.

We strike a bargain that if the Slusowskis pretend that they saw the paper later, I will not let on that I know how things really stand.

I then bid Kathy good-bye, promising to come by in the evening.

Then I run to the Art Institute. Through their good offices I will best be able to communicate with the management of the Salon Exhibition.

III

I send a telegram stating that I accept Baron Hirsh's terms, but first the painting is to be exhibited in Warsaw and so on.

Money for the telegram and other expenses is advanced to me from the Institute's treasury. They hand it over without hesitation. All is going swimmingly.

The *Flyer* and the *Pole* both publish my biography, which, by the way, contains not one word of truth. But as Ostrzynski says, "Why should I worry about details!"

I also receive offers from two illustrated magazines. They wish to publish my portrait and a reproduction of my painting.

Good, there will be money aplenty!

IV

A week later I pick up the deposit from Baron Hirsh. The remainder is to be paid when he takes possession of the canvas.

Meanwhile, the Commercial Bank pays out five thousand franks in solid gold. I return home loaded down like a mule.

There is a meeting in the studio. I dump my booty on the floor, and as I have never rolled in gold before, commence to do so.

After me, Swiatecki takes a turn at it.

The landlord enters and becomes convinced that we have lost our minds. Our amusement borders on the barbaric!

V

Ostrzynski tells me one day that he feels happy that Kathy had rejected him. He says that before him are possibilities about which I cannot even dream.

I am glad, but really it makes no difference, as I am convinced that Ostrzynski will be able to cope with life under most circumstances.

When he was courting Kathy the parents were on his side, especially old Slusowski. Ostrzynski held complete sway over him, even to such extent that Slusowski lost his Roman stature. Kathy, on the other hand, could not stand him from their first meeting. It was an unconscious dislike, and I am quite sure that she was not annoyed by the same facets of his personality that annoy me and those who know him better.

He is a strange person, and even a stranger literary figure.

Every literary and artistic circle has people in it about whom all wonder, "Whence their prestige?"

My friend, the editor of the *Flyer*, is one of these. Who would suspect that the secret of Ostrzynski's position and literary sway is the fact that he has no respect for talent—especially literary—and lives ignoring such. For them, he has the contempt of a man for whom a certain standard of living, an inbred cleverness, and a great amount of wit assure unfought-for victories in the social arena.

One should see him at literary meetings and dinners, how with jesting irony he treats people whose talents surpass his own tenfold. He presses them to the wall, confuses them with his logic, and then overwhelms them with his literary might.

Swiatecki, whenever I mention this, calls for a blunt instrument with which to smash Ostrzynski's head. But his prestige does not surprise me. Truly talented people are often timid, uncertain, and retiring. Yet, when the true talent finds itself alone, it soars. Under similar circumstances, Ostrzynski probably falls asleep, for there is nothing for him to ponder.

The future will right things, however, merit will assign rank. Ostrzynski has the intelligence to know this, but in his soul he mocks it. It is enough for him that for the moment, he is reckoned with more than his betters.

We painters are in his way. For writers, he sometimes will make allowances, as long as it fits in with the *Flyer*'s competition with the *Pole*.

But he is a pleasant companion and a fine human being. I could say that I like him but…

May the devil take Ostrzynski—enough of him.

VI

I am so disgusted that, one day soon, I shall slam the door.

What a farce! From the time I have acquired fame and money, Slusowski, counter to my expectations, treats me with positive disdain. He, his wife, and all the relatives turn a cold shoulder in my direction.

The very first evening Slusowski proclaimed that if I thought that my new position will influence their actions toward me, or if I thought, as he could see from my expression, that I am doing him a favor, then, though they are willing to sacrifice much for the good of their child, their only child cannot ask them to sacrifice their dignity. The mother added that the child knows full well where to find shelter.

Kathy attempts to defend me, sometimes very aggressively, but they wait upon my every word.

As soon as I open my mouth Slusowski bites his lower lip as if to say, "I knew it would end this way!" The farce goes on from morning till night.

And to think that all of this is hypocrisy, and that this is what is supposed to hold me in the trap, but in reality they are crowing to my fifteen thousand and are as anxious as I am, but for a different reason.

It is time to end it.

They are beginning to make me feel as if getting a gold medal and fifteen thousand franks was a heinous crime.

VII

The day of our formal engagement arrives.

I had purchased a fine Louis XV style ring which immediately fell into disfavor with the Slusowskis. Even

Kathy was not totally pleased. It seems that no one in the house has any idea what art is.

I must work on Kathy to eradicate some of there bourgeois notions and implant artistic ones. I am of good cheer, for, after all, she loves me.

To the engagement ceremony I decided to bring Swiatecki only. I had wanted to bring him to the Slusowskis for a visit earlier, but he had decided that as a moral and physical bankrupt he had not yet fallen so low as to "go calling." There was no solution.

I tried to prepare my future parents-in-law by explaining that my friend was a true original, a genius of a painter, and the most kindhearted man on earth.

Slusowski, learning that my friend paints "stiffs," raised his eyebrows and informed me that up to this time he had dealt with proper people only, that his career as a civil servant was unblemished, and that he hoped that Mr. Swiatecki would honor the customs that reign in an honest and humble household.

Inwardly, I am not altogether free from apprehension, therefore from dawn's break I am at war with Swiatecki. He stubbornly insists on wearing his trouser legs inside his boots. I persuade, plead, beg.

Finally he agrees by telling me that there is no reason why he should not play the fool. Too bad, for his shoes resemble those of Central African explorers. Bootblack has not touched them since they were bought, on credit, at the shoemaker's. What can I do!

Worse yet, Swiatecki's head resembles a mountain top covered by a forest recently devastated by a tornado. I must reconcile myself, for the rake to straighten out that rat's nest has yet to be forged.

Instead, I manage to force him into wearing a frock coat in place of his coarse peasant shirt. He puts on the frock but his face resembles that of one of his models. His disposition is morbid as well.

On the street people stare at his large knotty walking stick and his huge tattered hat but I am already used to that.

The bell rings, we enter.

The voice of cousin Jaczkowicz reaches us in the hall. He is preaching about overpopulation. Cousin Jaczkowicz is always talking about overpopulation. It is his one wisdom.

Kathy resembles a cloud in her satin dress. She is beautiful. Slusowski is dressed formally in a tail coat, as are all the male relatives. The aunts are in silk.

Swiatecki's entrance creates an impression. They eye him with a certain uneasiness. He casts his eye about in a sinister manner then declares that he would not bother Mr. Slusowski with his presence were it not for the fact that Wladek was getting engaged or some such thing.

The "some such thing" goes over very badly. Slusowski straightens up with great dignity and asks what precisely Mr. Swiatecki means by that. "Mr." Swiatecki answers that it does not matter to him, but for Wladek he would even allow himself to be castrated, especially if he knew that it mattered to Mr. Slusowski.

My future father-in-law looks at his wife, at Kathy, and then at me while surprise and shock battle on his face.

Fortunately, he has the presence of mind to propose that I be introduced to the members of the family who have not yet made my acquaintance.

After the presentation, we sit.

Kathy is by my side, her hand in mine. The room is filled with people, but all are stiff and silent. The atmosphere weighs heavy.

Cousin Jaczkowicz returns to his lecture on overpopulation. My Swiatecki begins looking under the table. In the silence the voice of cousin Jaczkowicz drones louder and louder. One of his front teeth is missing, so that every time he pronounces an "s" a drawn out hiss is heard.

"The worst type of disaster could, with time, envelop Europe," says Jaczkowicz.

"Emigration..." someone butts in.

"Statistics show that emigration does not limit population growth."

Suddenly Swiatecki turns his fish-like eyes onto the speaker.

"Then we should institute Chinese customs," he tones in seriously.

"Begging your pardon, which Chinese customs?"

"Well, in China parents have the right to strangle incorrigible children, here then, children should have the right to strangle incorrigible parents!"

The boom has fallen! The couch groaned under the aunts. I am lost. Slusowski closes his eyes and remains speechless.

Silence.

Finally the shaky voice of my father-in-law-to-be breaks the tension.

"Surely sir, as a Christian..."

"And why should I be a Christian..." interrupts Swiatecki, shaking his head angrily.

A second thunderclap. The couch with the aunts starts to convulse and plunges into a bottomless pit. I feel the earth part under my feet.

All hope is lost.

Then the air is shattered by the sound of Kathy's crystal clear, bell-like laughter. After her, not knowing why, Jaczkowicz explodes with mirth, after him, also not knowing why…laugh I.

"Daddy…" calls out Kathy. "Wladek warned us that Mr. Swiatecki was original. Mr. Swiatecki is joking, and I know that he has a mother and is a good son to her!"

Devil that girl! Not only can she fib, but guess as well. Indeed, Swiatecki has a mother and is a good son to her.

The laughter and the above explanation create a diversion. A greater one is provided by the entrance of a servant carrying wine and cakes. It is the same concierge, now dressed in tails and masquerading as a butler, who stole my last three rubles. His gaze is fixed on the tray, the glass is tinkling, and he moves as if he were carrying a tumbler brimming with water.

I begin to fear that he will drop the load. Fortunately, my fears prove futile…

In a moment the glasses are filled and we proceed with the formal ceremony of engagement.

A juvenile cousin holds a porcelain tray with the two rings on it. Her eyes are bulging with curiosity. The ceremony gives her so much pleasure that she is literally jumping up and down. Slusowski rises, the remainder of the clan rises. I hear chairs scraping the floor.

Silence descends again. I overhear one of the matrons whispering that she had hoped that I would provide a "better" ring. Even with this cutting remark, the mood is so festive that the flies are dropping off the walls.

Slusowski begins to speak.

"My children, receive the blessings of your parents."

Kathy kneels. I kneel.

Oh, the expression that Swiatecki must be wearing on his face now. What an expression!

I dare not look at him. Instead, I concentrate on Kathy's dress which is creating a colorful spot on the faded red rug. The hands of Mr. and Mrs. Slusowski rest on our heads, after which my future father-in-law continues.

"My daughter, you have had the best example at home of what a wife should be, therefore, I do not have to tell you your duties. These, (I hope!) your husband will acquaint you with. But I turn to you, Mr. Magorski..."

Here follows a speech during which I count to one hundred and having reached that number I begin again. Slusowski the civil servant, Slusowski the father, Slusowski the Roman, takes the opportunity to empty his soul. The words: child, parents, duty, future, blessings, thorns, clean conscience—buzz about my ears like a swarm of hornets. They light on my head, sting the above-mentioned ears, the neck and shoulders.

My tie must be tight for I feel I am being stifled. I hear the sobbing of Mrs. Slusowski which saddens me for basically she is a good woman. I hear the rattle of the rings on the tray held by the fidgeting cousin. God Almighty, what an expression Swiatecki must have on his face now!

Finally we rise. The little cousin shoves the tray right up to my nose. The rings are exchanged.

Wow! I am engaged! I had imagined that this would be the end but Slusowski invites us to solicit the blessings of the maiden aunts.

We go. I kiss five sets of hands that resemble heron paws. The aunts hope that I will not disappoint their faith in me.

What kind of faith, in God's name, should they have in me? Cousin Jaczkowicz embraces me. Definitely, my tie must be too tight.

The worst is over. Dusk descends. Tea is brought in.

I sit by Kathy and try to pretend that Swiatecki does not exist. That ape fills me with apprehension once again when asked if he would like some brandy in his tea. He answers that he drinks brandy "only by the bottle."

Finally, the evening winds up successfully. We exit. I take a lungful of air. Indeed, my tie was too tight.

We walk in silence, a silence that begins to bother me. I feel that I should say something to Swiatecki, to tell him about my happiness, about how well it all went, how much I love Kathy. I try but it just won't go. Finally, near our lodgings, I blurt out, "You must admit that life can be beautiful sometimes."

Swiatecki stops, gives me one of his underhanded looks, and says… "Poodle!"

We spoke no more that evening.

VIII

A week after my engagement, my *Jews* arrived and were placed on exhibit.

The painting was placed in a separate room, with additional admission charged by the management. One half of the clear profit goes to me. Reportedly the exhibition hall is filled from dawn to dusk.

I went there once, but got stared at more than the painting. I will not go again. There is no use annoying myself unnecessarily.

Even if the painting were a masterpiece heretofore unseen on earth, the public would still wish to satisfy its curiosity in the same manner which they would use to inspect "Krao"—the Hottentot who swallows live doves.

Right now I am such a Hottentot. I would be more comfortable if I were a poodle. But I am too much of a painter to endure the degradation of art in the presence of a famous personality.

IX

Three weeks ago hardly anyone knew I existed, now I receive dozens of letters, of the "romantic" type for most part. Four out of five start with "Perhaps after reading this letter you will scorn a woman who…" I'll scorn no woman, as long as she leaves my soul alone.

If it weren't for Kathy, I would not be so indifferent to this outpouring of emotion.

The thing that annoys me most is how these women expect a reply from a man who has never seen them. Pull back the curtain, oh, lovely one, when I see you I'll tell you. Oh! I'll say nothing, for after all, there's Kathy.

I have also received a letter from a gray haired advisoress in which she calls me "the master," and Kathy "a goose."

"Master, is that a wife fit for you?" she writes. "Is that the choice of one upon whom the eyes of the nation are turned? You are the victim of intrigue, etc." *ad nauseam*.

A strange idea, and even stranger the demand that I marry to please public opinion rather than follow the promptings of my heart. Poor Kathy seems to be in everyone's way.

There are probably greater crimes than the writing of anonymous letters, but there is no greater… How to put it nicely? Oh well, never mind.

The date of our wedding is not yet set, but it will happen soon.

Let them see us together.

Swiatecki's "stiffs" have also arrived from Paris. The title of the painting is *Final Rendezvous*. It shows a boy and a girl lying side by side on an autopsy table. The theme is self-evident at first sight. It is clear that these two have loved each other in life, were separated by poverty, and reunited in death.

The students leaning over the corpses look a bit harsh. The perspective of the operating theater has some flaws, but the "stiffs" are perfect. So cold are they that an icy breeze seems to rise from the canvas. At the competition it took no prizes, probably due to the sad topic, but it got more than its share of critical praise.

In our own artistic circle there is, no doubt, a lot of talent. Right beside Swiatecki's painting Frank Cepkowski exhibited his *Death of a Polish Nobleman*. What power and individualism!

Swiatecki calls Frank an idiot because Cepkowski dresses fashionably, wears a goatee, long hair, is well brought up and courteous, and often alludes to his upper crust relations.

But Swiatecki is wrong.

Talent is a creature that resides wherever it likes, be it in an impenetrable jungle or a well groomed garden. In Munich and Paris I saw artists who resembled brewery hands or just the opposite—barbers and dandies.

I'd not give a wooden coin for the lot, yet there was some kind of exaltation in their souls combined with a feeling for color and the ability to get it out on canvas.

Ostrzynski, who has a ready expression for any situation would no doubt write in his Flyer: *Spiritus flat, ubi vult!* [The spirit dwells where it will].

In Swiatecki's opinion, historical painting is a "heinous barbarism." He does not paint historical subjects and while I don't care if he does or not, I hear that this point of view is "progressive." Someone already made a saw of it and it is beginning to bore me.

Our Polish painters have one major fault, they marry a doctrine and live under its heel. They survey all that they see through it, align their art to it, and are better apostles than painters.

I have met artists whose lips were frayed from deep philosophical discussions about the nature of art, what it should be and so on, but when it came to wielding a brush, they failed miserably.

Often I think that theories should be left to the philosophers—and should they make the theory stupid—let them answer for it.

Painters, however, should paint what they feel and should know how, for that is basic.

To me, the smallest talent is worth more than the greatest doctrine, and the greatest doctrine is not fit to shine freedom's shoes.

X

I took Kathy and the Slusowskis to the exhibit. There is always a crowd gathered around my painting.

Whispers started the minute we entered. But this time attention was diverted from me and the painting to Kathy. The women, especially, could not take their eyes off her.

She was absolutely enthralled by all this, and I could not hold it against her.

Worse that she called Swiatecki's "stiffs" an "indecent" painting. Slusowski swore that she snatched the words from his lips. This only enraged me. Oh! That Kathy could have such an outlook on art!

Concealing my anger, I bid them good-bye under the pretext that I had a luncheon engagement with Ostrzynski. Then I went to his office and dragged him out to a restaurant.

XI

I saw a miracle!

Now finally I know why men have eyes.

"Corpo di Baccho!" What a beauty!

I am walking along with Ostrzynski. Suddenly, on the corner, a woman passes us. I freeze. I am stupefied and petrified. With my eyes open I lose consciousness, grab Ostrzynski's tie and unknowingly undo it—for, help—I am lost!

What if her features are excellent, features—next to none. She is nothing else than an artistic idea! A masterpiece as a sketch, a masterpiece as an oil, a masterpiece as a sentiment. Greuze would probably be resurrected by the sight of her and then promptly hang himself for painting such hags.

I look and look. She walks alone, yet not alone. With her walks poetry, music, spring, love, and delight! I do not know if I should paint her portrait immediately or throw myself at her feet and kiss them for being born so. But then, do I really know what I want.

She passes us, peaceful as a summer day. Ostrzynski bows to her, but she does not seem to notice him. I wake from my daze and begin to shout. "Let's follow her!"

"No," answers Ostrzynski, "are you crazy? I must re-tie my tie. Give me some peace. She is a friend."

"Your friend? Introduce me!"

"I would not think of it. Take care of your own fiancée."

I put a pox on Ostrzynski and his progeny to the ninth generation, then I want to chase after the lovely stranger. Unfortunately, she boards a carriage.

In the distance I see her straw hat and parasol.

"Do you really know her?" I query Ostrzynski.

"I know everyone."

"Who is she?"

"She is Madame Helen Kolczanowski, from the family of Turno, also known as the 'Maiden Widow'."

"Why 'Maiden Widow'?"

"Because her husband died at the wedding banquet. If you have recovered sufficiently I'll tell you the story.

"There was an old, but very wealthy bachelor, Kolc-zanowski de Kolczano, an Ukrainian noble. He had an extremely large family, which expected to inherit, and an extremely short neck which gave great hopes to the inheritors. I knew them, quite decent people really, but human nature is what it is. Even the best, the least in-terested, could not resist staring at Kolczanowski's short neck. This annoyed him so much that, to spite the family he proposed to the neighbor's daughter, changed his will making her sole heir, and then got married. A dinner fol-lowed the wedding. Right after the dessert an apoplectic fit finished him off. Thus, Madame Helen became the 'Maiden Widow'."

"When was this?"

"Three years ago. She was twenty-two then. Since then she could have been married twenty-two times. Some thought she was waiting for a prince. This assumption proved wrong, as she rejected one just recently. I know well that there are no pretensions, the best proof of this is her friendship with our talented, well-known actress, Eve Adami, whom she has known since school."

Hearing this I nearly jumped for joy.

If this is so then Ostrzynski can soak his head. My dear, kind Eve will introduce me to Madame Kolczanowski.

"Listen, will you take me to her?" I ask Ostrzynski.

"In the end, if you want to meet someone in this town— you will," he answers, "but you took Kathy away from me, well, I would not want it said that I was responsible. But, what do I know… Good Day!"

XII

I was supposed to be at the Slusowskis for dinner, but I wrote that I could not make it.

My teeth have not hurt me a day in my life, but there was no reason for them not to start.

I could not forget Helen. Her face was before me the whole day, for is there an artist that would not ponder over such a face?

In my soul I painted her ten portraits. Then I got an idea for a painting in which Helen's face would create a sensation. All I had to do was to see her just a few more times.

I ran over to Eve's, but did not find her at home. In the evening I received an invitation from Kathy asking that I join them for a morning walk in the park to take the waters, followed by coffee. It's becoming a regular routine with the park, the "waters," and that damned coffee!

I can't go, for if I don't catch Eve in the morning, then I won't see her for the entire day.

Eve Adami (that is a stage name, the real one being Anne Jedlinski), is an exceptional person. We have been friends for a long time and are on a strict first name basis.

It has been five years since she entered the theater and she has remained pure in the full meaning of the word. In the theater there are, no doubt, many women who are physically innocent, but should the corsets choose to reveal the doings of their mistress, I imagine that even the most cocksure lothario would turn red in all the places not covered with fur. The theater ruins souls, especially the feminine.

It is difficult to demand that a woman who each evening portrays love, loyalty, nobility, etc. would not, after a while, begin to feel instinctively that those virtues are mere tinsel, belonging strictly to the stage and having little to do with reality.

The great difference between art and the reality of life can be expressed in this vein—competition and the desire for recognition poison the nobler motives of the heart.

The constant exposure to people as corrupted as actors will start anyone thinking. There is no white angora cat that would not get sullied under similar circumstances. Only a great talent can be victorious over such influence, one that purifies by its own flame, or a nature so thoroughly esthetic that evil cannot penetrate it, just as a swan's feathers repel water. Eve Adami is one such "impermeable."

We have spent many long evenings over pipe and tea discussing the people who belong to the world of art. We would start with the highest category—poets, and finish with actors—the lowest.

What is an artist but a creature more sensitive than others, more intellectual, more spontaneous, one knowing the limits of passion and pleasure, and desiring it all with unlimited strength.

An artist, therefore, should have more character and willpower than others to resist the temptations of life.

Unfortunately, just as there is no reason that a beautiful flower should be more resistant to the elements than a weed, so it is with artists. There is no reason that they should have more character than an ordinary mortal.

Often it is just the reverse, however, for an artist usually has less moral fortitude, as his strength is sapped from battling in the chasm that separates the daily world from the world of art.

An artist is akin to a feverish bird, sometimes soaring among the clouds, sometimes dragging its wings in the dust. Art gives him a distaste for the dust, yet daily life takes away the strength to fly. Such is the separation between the inner and public life of an actor.

The world which asks more of them than of others may be right in castigating them, but Christ will be right as well, when he saves them.

Ostrzynski, on the other hand, holds that actors belong to the artistic world the same way as trombones, clarinets, viols belong to music. But this viewpoint has no merit.

The best proof of this is Eve Adami, who is the personification of an artist through her talent and artistic feeling—which has preserved her from harm like a mother.

In spite of our long friendship I had not seen her in a long while, so seeing me caused her great happiness, even though the expression on her face perplexed me.

"How are you Wladek," she said. "Well here you are!"

I was quite happy to have caught up with her.

She wore a Turkish robe, cream colored with red spots, a wide border and slit sleeves. The dark border contrasted especially well with her pale complexion and blue eyes. I told her so, which made her glad, then got down to business.

"My golden one," I continue, "do you know Madame Kolczanowski, the beautiful Ukrainian?"

"I know her, she is an old friend."

"Take me to her…"

She begins to shake her head.

"My golden one, my beautiful one, is that how you love me?"

"No, Wladek, I will not take you to her."

"And you see, you are so cruel, and I nearly fell in love with you."

That Eve is such a mimosa.

Hearing this she changes her countenance and rests her shapely elbows on the table, placing her chin on her palms.

"When was this?"

I am in a hurry to talk about Helen, but, really, once I almost did fall in love with Eve. Now, wanting to put her in a good mood I tell her the story.

"It was like this. After the theater we took a walk in the botanical gardens. Remember, the night was gorgeous! We sat on a bench near the pond, you said you wanted to hear the nightingale sing. I was a little sad, my hat was off, my head splitting with a headache. You walked over to the pond, dipped your best handkerchief in the water and pressed it to my forehead. At that moment you were an angel to me, and I thought that if I took that little hand and pressed it to my lips I would fall in love forever."

"And?"

"Suddenly you drew back as if you had sensed something."

Eve sat for a while in a quiet study, then recovered and added in a nervous rush, "Let us not speak of this, please."

"Very well, we won't talk about it. You know, Eve, I like you too much to ever fall in love with you. One precludes the other. From the time I have met you I have felt nothing but a true friendship toward you."

"But," adds Eve as if following another train of thought, "is it not true that you are engaged?"

"True."

"Why did you not tell me about it?"

"For it was off, but has been renewed recently. But if you tell me that as an engaged man I should not try to make the acquaintance of Madame Kolczanowski, then hear this—I was a painter before I was a fiancé. Besides, you have nothing to fear from me."

"I would not think of it. To take you to her would make her the object of general gossip. For the last several weeks I have been hearing that half of Warsaw is in love with you. The stories of your conquests are incredible. As late as yesterday, I had heard it said in jest that from God's ten commandments you had made yourself one."

"And what commandment is that?"

"Thou shalt not covet thy neighbor's wife…in vain."

"Oh, lord, look at my misery! But the joke is good."

"And no doubt to the point."

"Listen Eve, do you want to know the truth? I was always shy and retiring, especially when it came to women. People imagine God knows what, but believe me, you have no idea of how much truth there was in my exclamation, 'Lord, look at my misery!'"

"*Povero Maestro!*"

"Oh, cut out the Italian. Will you take me to Madame Kolczanowski?"

"I can't, dear Wladek. As long as you pass for a Don Juan it would not be proper for me, an actress, to lead you to an unmarried woman as desirable as Helen."

"Well, why did you receive me then?"

"I am different. As an actress, I can apply Shakespeare's words to my position, 'Be thou as chaste as ice, as pure as snow, thou shall not escape calumny!'"

"But, you know, one can lose one's mind. It seems that anyone can meet her, look at her, except me. Why? Because I painted a good picture and gained a certain measure of fame for it."

"You are right on that point," Eve agrees, smiling. "Don't think that I did not know you were coming. Ostrzynski was here telling me that I had 'better' not take you to her."

"Oh, I understand. Then you promised."

"I promised nothing, I even got mad at him. But I think that I had 'better' not take you. Let's talk about your painting."

"Oh, forget the painting! Very well! I'm telling you that in three days time I will make the acquaintance of Madame Kolczanowski even if I have to go to her in disguise!"

"Dress as a gardener and take her a bouquet...from Ostrzynski."

At that moment I am struck with an idea, so incredibly delicious that I strike my forehead. I forget the slight resentment I had felt toward Eve. I am hardly able to contain myself.

"Give me your word that you will not betray me."

"Given," answers Eve, becoming interested.

"Listen, I will dress myself as an Ukrainian lyrist, a *lirnik*, I have the costume and a lyre. I have been to Ukraine and can sing the songs. Madame Kolczanowski cannot but receive me. Understand…"

"What an original idea!"

She is too much of an artist not to like the idea, and she gave me her word. She cannot object.

"What an original idea," she repeats. "Helen loves her Ukraine so that she will probably cry when she sees a lyrist here in Warsaw. But how will you explain how you got here?"

My enthusiasm infects Eve. After a while we sit and plot in earnest.

We reach an agreement. I will disguise myself, and Eve will pick me up in a carriage, as not to attract too much attention from gapers. Madame Helen will not know anything until Eve decides to reveal our secret.

We enjoy our game enormously. Finally, I kiss her hand to leave, but she insists on my staying for lunch.

The evening I spend at the Slusowskis.

Kathy is a little annoyed that I did not come in the morning, but I take her moods like an angel, thinking all the while about tomorrow's expedition…and Helen.

XIII

It is eleven in the morning.

Eve should be here soon.

I am dressed in a coarse peasant shirt, open across the chest. The remainder of my outfit is a bit worn but proper—belt, boots, all that is necessary.

The hair of a silver gray wig falls over my forehead, and he would be wise who could tell that it was a wig. My beard is a tribute to patience. As of eight in the morning, I had been adding, with the help of a stiff paste, white hairs in between my own. As a result I aged so naturally that time could not have done better. Some thinned sepia gave me a swarthy complexion, while Swiatecki executed the wrinkles in an absolutely brilliant way. I look at least seventy years old.

Swiatecki proposed that instead of painting, I should earn my bread as a model, which he insisted would be an even greater contribution to art.

At eleven-thirty Eve arrives.

I send down a bundle which contains my regular street clothes. I don't know if I'll have need of them. Then I grab my lyre and descend. I greet her at the door with *"Slawa Bohu!"*

Adami is surprised and thrilled.

"Beautiful belt, beautiful *lirnik!*" she repeats laughing. "Only an artist could dream up such a thing!"

Speaking aside, she resembles a summer morning. I can't take my eyes off her raw silk dress, and the straw hat decorated with poppies. She arrived in an open carriage, a crowd of onlookers starts to gather. This does not bother her in the least.

Finally, the carriage departs. My heart beats faster and faster—only a quarter of an hour to seeing Helen.

We did not go one hundred yards before I noticed Ostrzynski coming down the street.

This one must be everywhere!

Seeing Eve, he stops and bows. Then he begins to appraise us both with a firm stare, especially me. I do not think that he recognized me, but after we pass, he continues to stand and stare. Fortunately, we turn a corner and lose him. The carriage moves swiftly, yet the trip seems to last centuries. At last we pull up at the head of Belvedere Avenue.

We are in front of Helen's house. I run to the door like a madman. Eve chases me shouting, "Oh, what a naughty old man!"

A fancily dressed servant opens the door. His eyes bulge at the sight of me. Eve calms him by explaining that I am her charge. We proceed upstairs.

A maid appears for a moment and announces that Madame is dressing in an adjoining room. Then she vanishes.

"Good day!" Eve calls out.

"Good day, Eve!" answers an incredibly fresh voice. "Just one minute, I will be ready in a moment."

"Helen! You have no idea who I've got here to see you—as genuine a *lirnik* as has ever walked the Ukrainian steppes!"

I hear a joyful shriek from the next room, and then Helen dashes in sans dress, just corset and unfurled hair.

"A *lirnik*, a blind *lirnik* here in Warsaw?"

"Not blind, he can see!" shouts Eve, not wishing to take the thing too far.

But it is too late, for in that moment I throw myself at Helen's feet with a shout.

"Cherubim of God!" I embrace her feet paying strict attention to the ankles. Nations kneel, peoples bring tribute, she is absolutely incomparable!

"Cherubim!," I repeat my greeting with genuine emotion.

My enthusiasm can be explained by the fact that after my long wanderings I have finally come upon another Ukrainian soul. For a brief instant, I see her bare shoulders and neck, reminiscent of Psyche from the Neapolitan museum. Then she disappears leaving me in a prone position in the center of the floor.

Eve shakes her parasol at me and simultaneously hides her laughter by putting her nose into a bouquet of violets.

Meanwhile, a conversation begins through the door. It is carried on in the most beautiful Ukrainian dialect that I have ever heard.

I had prepared myself for all and any questions, so I lie like a saint. I am a serf from Czeheryn. My daughter married a hussar from the Warsaw regiment. Loneliness got the better of me, so I followed. Good people gave me coins for my songs. And now? I'll see the little ones, bless them and return for I miss mother Ukraine. There I will die, in the orchards among the beehives. All must die and it is past time for old Fylyp.

What a nature actors have. Eve knows full well what is going on, yet she is so taken by my story that she begins to nod her head sadly and give me sympathetic looks. Helen's voice acquires an emotional tone as well.

The door opens a crack, a beautiful arm appears, then suddenly I find myself the possessor of a three ruble note which I am forced to accept, for I cannot do otherwise. In return, I call upon all the saints to send a veritable torrent of blessings upon Helen's head.

I am interrupted by the same maid whom we saw earlier. She announces that Mr. Ostrzynski is at the door.

"Don't let him in, dear!" cautions Eve, a bit frightened.

Helen declares that she will not see him. Moreover, she expresses surprise at such an early visit. I also am puzzled as to how Ostrzynski, who prides himself on his knowledge of etiquette, could call so early.

"There is something to this," says Eve.

But there is no time for explanations, for Helen is ready and brunch is announced.

Helen wants me to sit at the table, but I am stubborn and sit, together with my lyre, in the doorway. In a moment I am given a bowl filled with food sufficient to give six Ukrainian peasants indigestion. Being hungry, I eat and cast occasional long glances at Helen.

Truly, there is no head like hers in any gallery. In my life I have never seen such translucent eyes. One can almost see the thoughts of the owner, right down to the conscience. Those eyes have the additional property of smiling before the lips do, and brighten the face like a ray of sunlight. There is an incredible sweetness in the lines of her lips—she seems to be a composition by the finest masters.

Finally, I finish eating and just stare—I could continue to my dying day.

"You did not visit me yesterday," says Helen to Eve. "I thought you were going to drop in."

"I had a rehearsal in the morning, and in the afternoon I wanted to see Magorski's painting."

"Did you see it?"

"Not well…there was such a crush. How about you?"

"I went in the morning. What a poet! I wanted to cry with those Jews."

Eve looks at me. My soul is glowing.

"I'll go again, as often as I can," Helen continues. "Why don't we go together? Maybe even today. It was a great pleasure to see that painting, and to think that there is such a talent among us."

How can one not worship such a woman?

Then I hear more—"It is unfortunate that such strange things are being said about him. I must admit that I am dying to meet him."

"Ach!" says Eve carelessly.

"You know him, don't you?"

"I can assure you that his personality loses much at close range. He is arrogant and vain, oh, so vain!"

I get the urge to stick my tongue out at Eve, I can hardly hold back.

She turns her roughish eyes to me and says, "Lose your appetite, grandpa?"

I'll stick my tongue out, I just can't stand it!

Then to Helen, "It is better to admire him than to meet him in person. Ostrzynski describes him as a genius in the body of an oaf."

I would tear Ostrzynski's ears off if he dared to say such a thing. I knew that Eve had mischief lurking behind her collar, but this surpasses all measure.

Finally, we finish.

We walk into the garden where I am to perform.

I am getting a little bored with the whole thing. I would rather be here as a painter than a *lirnik*. Unfortunately, there is no solution to the situation.

I sit by a wall in the shade of chestnut trees. The sun is breaking through the leaves and forms a jumble of bright spots on the ground. These spots vibrate, glitter, disappear and reappear as the breeze rustles the leaves. The garden gives the impression of a depth where normal city noises do not penetrate. What noise does pass through is masked by the gurgling of a small fountain. The heat is great. Somewhere in the branches, sparrows chirp, but they sound weak and sleepy. The rest is silence.

I can see how all this forms a beautiful composition. The garden, the trees, the fountain, two women, their faces uncommonly beautiful, and I with my lyre against the wall. All this has a charm, which I, as a painter, can sense.

I partly forget about the playacting and begin to sing.

> *They say that I am blessed,*
> *Free of worries and fears.*
> *They fail to see how often,*
> *I weep a sea of tears.*
>
> *Unfortunate I was born,*
> *Unfortunate I'll die.*
> *Why, mother, did you birth me?*
> *Why?—each dark night I cry.[6]*

Eve is moved by it because she is an artist, Helen because she is Ukrainian, I because they are beautiful. The very sight is a pleasure to behold.

Helen listens without any pretense, there are no feigned emotions, yet in her translucent eyes I can see the intense pleasure she draws from it.

What a difference there is between her and Ukrainian girls who come to Warsaw to take part in the festivals. While dancing they bore their partners with tales of their longing for Ukraine. In truth, wild horses would not suffice to drag them back to their "beloved" homeland.

Helen listens, keeping time with her elegant head. Sometimes she whispers to Eve, "I know that," and then sings along with me. I seem to surpass myself in

---

6   The song was translated from Ukrainian by Dr. Leo Rudnycky and his son Nicholas.

the performance. My memory unearths a vast store of material. I cover the range from Hetmans, Uhlans, and Cossacks to Sonias, Marysias and God knows what else. I have absolutely no idea where I got it all from.

Time passes like a dream.

I return home tired but intoxicated.

XIV

In the studio, to my amazement, I find Kathy and her parents.

They wanted to surprise me!

Why on earth did Swiatecki tell them that I would be back soon?

Kathy and her parents do not recognize me. Proof to the quality of my disguise. I approach Kathy and take her hand. Frightened, she pulls it back.

"Kathy, don't you recognize me?" I ask.

I can't help but laugh at their surprise.

"Why, it's Wladek!" shouts Swiatecki.

Kathy inspects me closely, and begins to laugh, "Foo, what an ugly old man!"

So I'm an ugly old man. I'd like to know where she saw a prettier one. But to Kathy, brought up on the esthetic principles of papa Slusowski, all old men are no doubt ugly.

I duck into the kitchen and a moment later emerge in my usual form.

Kathy and her parents begin to question me about the "masquerade."

"What was the masquerade about? Well…it's a perfectly simple thing… You see…well…painters do favors for each other by posing as models for paintings. See…

for example, Swiatecki posed as the old Jew in my painting. Didn't you recognize him Kathy? Now I'm posing for Cepkowski. It is a custom among painters, especially with the shortage of models in Warsaw."

"We came to surprise you," says Kathy, "and I have never seen a studio before. Oh, what disorder. Is it like this with all painters?"

"More or less, more or less."

Mr. Slusowski proclaims that he expects to see a change in the future. I get the desire to crack my lyre against his skull. Kathy, however, gets into a coquettish mood and says, "There's one mister painter whose ways will change. When I start working all will be dusted, straightened, put away."

So saying she points her nose upward where festooned cobwebs decorate the corners of the studio.

Then she adds, "Even a junk dealer would not stand such disorder. Take this armor, oh! how rusty. All I have to do is call the scullery maid, have her break up some brick and it will shine like a new samovar."

Jesus H. Christ! She talks about junkmen and wants to clean my precious armor plate which I have just lately snitched from the graveyard. Oh, Kathy, Kathy!

Her father, joyfully relieved, kisses her forehead while Swiatecki is giving out warlike grunts reminiscent of a charging boar.

Kathy waves her little finger in front of my nose and continues, "Remember, all must change." Then she finishes with, "There's one mister painter whom we won't love if he doesn't come in the evening." So saying, she bats her eyelids.

I can't say I detect anything pleasant in these frills. I promise that I'll come and lead the family downstairs.

On my return I find Swiatecki eyeing a bundle of banknotes in distrust.

"What is this?"

"Do you know what happened?"

"No."

"I robbed a man, just like a common thief."

"How so?"

"I sold my painting."

"And that's the money."

"Yes, and I am a stinking cheat!"

I embrace him, congratulating him with all my heart. Then he tells me how it happened.

"I was sitting here after you departed, when in comes a gentleman and asks if I am Swiatecki. I answer 'I'd be interested in knowing why I should not be Swiatecki!' So he says, 'I saw your painting and I would like to buy it.' So I say, 'One would have to be an idiot to buy such a vile painting.' And he to that, 'An idiot I am not, but I do fancy paintings done by idiots.' 'If so, then, very well,' I said. He asks for a price but I tell him not to worry about it too much. He names a price. I agree. If he wants to toss his money into the gutter, it's fine by me. He left the money and went. Here is his card, Dr. W. Bialkowski, M.D. I'm just a foul cheat!"

"Long live the 'stiffs,' Swiatecki, get married…"

"I'd rather hang myself," he broods, "I'm nothing but the vilest of cheats!"

XV

I spend the evening at the Slusowskis.

Kathy and I have found a place in the foyer where a love seat stands in an alcove.

Mrs. Slusowski is sewing by the light of a lamp, something for Kathy's trousseau, no doubt. Mr. Slusowski is reading the evening issue of the *Flyer* by the light of the same lamp.

I feel strange somehow and try to overcome this feeling by moving closer to Kathy. The foyer is quiet, only Kathy's whisper, as I try to embrace her, disturbs the peace.

"Papa will see."

At that point "papa" takes to voice and begins to read loudly. "The painting, *Last Rendezvous* by the well known artist, Anthony Swiatecki, was purchased today by Dr. Bialkowski, M.D. for 5,000 rubles."

"Yes," I add, "he sold it this morning."

At that point I once again try to embrace Kathy. Again she protests. "Papa will see."

Reflexively my eyes turn to Mr. Slusowski. Suddenly, I see that his expression is changing. He shields his eyes as he leans closer to the printed page.

What in God's name could he have found so interesting.

"Father, what is it?" asks his wife.

He rises, walks two steps toward me, stops, cuts me in two with a glaring stare, and wringing his hands he begins to nod his head.

"What is the matter?"

"This is how lies and deception come to light!" he answers pathetically. "Here, my dear sir, read this if your shame permits you to finish!"

So saying, with a motion that resembles the wrapping of a toga, he hands me the paper. I take it. My eyes behold an article entitled *The Ukrainian Lyrist.* I am incredibly confounded, but go on to read the following:

As of several days ago our fair city has been graced by an extraordinary guest in the person of an elderly lyrist who has been touring the houses of Ukrainian families begging alms and giving song in return. It is said that the old bard's patroness is none other than E.A., our well-known and kindhearted actress in whose carriage he has been seen just this morning. Since the first days of his appearance a rumor has spread that under that coarse and simple tunic was none other than one of our finest painters, who in this manner, without arousing the suspicions of husbands or guardians, found an easy access to the boudoirs. We are sure, however, that there is no basis to this rumor for the very reason that our "diva" would never sanction such behavior. The oldster, according to reliable sources, marched here straight from Ukraine. His reason is somewhat dim, but his memory is excellent…

Hell!

Slusowski is so beside himself with rage that he cannot utter a word. Finally, he throws out a scrap of his fury.

"What new lie, what new deception will you fabricate to justify this behavior? Was it not you whom we saw in that shameful costume? Who on earth is that man?"

"I am that man," I answer, "but I do not understand why you call the costume shameful."

In that moment, Kathy snatches the *Flyer* from my hands and starts to read hungrily. Slusowski wraps himself more securely in his toga of indignation and continues.

"Well, even when you first crossed the threshold of a decent house, you brought degradation with you. Even without being the husband of this unhappy child, already you have betrayed her in the company of women of easy virtue. Already you tread on out trust, break your word—for whom—a theatrical harlot!"

Uncontrollable anger grips me in a steely hold.

"My dear sir," I spout, "enough of these speeches! That…harlot is worth a dozen pharisees like you! In addition, know sir that you are a bore! I have had enough of your preaching, enough of your…"

I run out of words. Really, I do not want to say anything else. Slusowski opens his vest as if to say, "Strike, here I am."

I have no intention of striking. I just want to leave after making it clear that I am doing so as not to have to tell Mr. Slusowski anything more about himself.

I exit without as much as a good-bye.

The night breeze cools my burning forehead.

It is nine in the evening and the night is very calm. I need to unwind so I decide to take a walk. I head in the direction of Belvedere Avenue.

The windows of Helen's house are dark. Obviously, she is not at home. I don't know why but this makes me tremendously sad.

If I had seen her shadow in a window, I would have felt better. As it is a new wave of anger hits me.

I don't know what I'll do to Ostrzynski the next time I see him.

Fortunately, he is not a man who shirks responsibility.

Only, to make a point, what will I pick on? The article is written with devilish cleverness. Ostrzynski disavows that the lyrist was a painter in disguise. He seems to defend Eve, but at the same time reveals the secret to Helen. Obviously, he is trying to compromise Eve before Helen. He takes revenge on me for Kathy, and makes me out to be a ridiculous fool.

Oh, if he only had not written that my reason was dim! Oh well, I must seem funny to Helen now. She, of course, reads the *Flyer*.

Oh, what a mess, and what an insult to Eve! How triumphant Ostrzynski must be now. Something must be done, and if I could have my way I think I would become a reporter for the *Flyer*.

I get the idea that this might be a good time to confer with Eve. She is giving a performance tonight. I'll dash over to the theater and catch her after the play.

There is still time.

Half an hour later I am in her dressing room.

Eve will be done shortly. Meanwhile, I pause to have a look around.

Our theaters are not known for their luxurious furnishings. The room is a cubicle with four whitewashed walls. Two gas jets sway in the draft, a mirror, a washstand, several chairs, and a couch, probably the personal property of the actress, comprise the furnishings. In front of the mirror is an assortment of makeup articles, a partly consumed cup of coffee, boxes of face powder, eyebrow pencils, several pairs of gloves—still retaining the shape of a woman's hand—a set of braids, such is her dressing room. On the wall hangs a number of gowns—white, pink, dark, light, heavy. Two baskets on the floor brim full of womanly accessories. The air is permeated with the aroma of powder and rouge. What a clash of color everywhere. How all this is spread about in a frantic hurry! The colors, reflections and shadows play in the motion of the gas jets.

It is a work of art in its own right. There is character here. Really, there is nothing more here than in any woman's dressing room, except for a certain magical charm.

Over the disorder, between the scarred walls, hovers the spirit of art.

I hear the thunder of applause. Well, it's over. Through the wall I hear shouts "Adami! Adami!" A quarter of an hour passes and still they scream.

Finally, Eve bursts in as *Queen Theodora*. A crooked tiara adorns her head. Her eyes are heavily shaded, a rouge blush covers her cheeks.

Her unbraided hair falls about her bare neck and shoulders. She is excited and exhausted to such a point that she can speak only in a faint whisper.

"How are you Wladek?"

Then taking off the tiara, she throws herself on the couch in her majestic gown. She cannot utter a word, she only looks at me in silence—just like a tired bird. I sit by her, put my hand on her forehead and think of nothing but her.

I can see that in those made-up eyes the fires of emotion have not died out yet. I can almost see the stigma on her forehead. I can see how this girl brings to the altar of the theatrical Moloch health, blood, and life until there is barely a breath left in her body. I am seized by such pity, such sympathy, such understanding, that I really don't know what to do.

We sit in silence for a while. Finally, Eve points to a copy of the *Flyer* on the floor.

"What a pity, what a shame," she gasps.

Then she bursts out in tears, shaking like a leaf.

I know that this was brought on by exhaustion, not by anything printed in the *Flyer*. The article is a mere trifle to be forgotten tomorrow. Ostrzynski is not worth one of Eve's tears, but still my heart grieves. I take her hands and after kissing them, hold them close to me. My heart starts beating faster and then a strange thing happens. I kneel at her feet, a haze seems to cover my sight, Then suddenly and recklessly, not knowing what I am doing I take her in my arms.

"Wladek, have mercy," whispers Eve.

But I press her to my body without thought, madly. I kiss her face, her forehead, her lips. On my own lips is but one phrase, "I love you, I love you!"

Then Eve's head tilts back, her arms encircle my neck and I hear her whisper, "I have loved you for such a long time."

XVI

If there is a creature in this world that is dearer to me than Eve then I'm a marinated herring.

It is said that we, artists, do everything on impulse, but it is not so. It appears that I have loved Eve for a long time, but was too much of a jackass to know it.

God knows what happened to me when I walked her home that evening. We went hand in hand without saying a word. I held her hand tightly to my body, and she held mine to hers. Finally, when she lifted her hand to her face, did I awake.

"Eve, is it true you are mine?"

"Yes, yes!"

She was beautiful, her eyes sleepy, yet shiny, and such a sweet disposition that I could hardly break away.

In truth she did not want to part from me either, as if to make up for the long silence and repressed feelings.

I returned home late. Swiatecki was not in bed. He was sketching on wood by the light of a lamp.

"There's a letter here for you," he said without lifting his eyes from his work.

In picking up the envelope I could feel the ring inside. Good! I'll need it tomorrow. I opened the envelope and read.

> I know that the return of this ring will cause you some pleasure for, obviously, that is what you desired. As for me, I would not think to rival an actress. K.

Well, at least it was short.

The letter communicates anger, nothing more.

If there ever was an aura surrounding Kathy, it fades irrecoverably. Strange thing, everyone thought that Eve was the cause of my disguising myself and all the deceptions. Instead, she is the cause of what will happen next.

I dispose of the letter, pocket the ring and go to bed.

Swiatecki looks up from his work expecting a statement. I offer none.

"That lousy Ostrzynski was here this evening, right after the theater," he said.

XVII

The next morning I want to run over to see Eve, but I can't as I have visitors.

Baron Kartofler drops in and orders a copy of my painting. He wants to give me fifteen hundred rubles. I hold out for two-thousand. An agreement is struck.

After his departure, Tanzenberg orders two portraits. Swiatecki, a confirmed anti-Semite, begins to mouth off about Jewish painters. But I'd be interested to know who would buy works of art if not "financiers." If they are afraid of Swiatecki's "stiffs," it is not my fault.

I make it over to Eve's at one in the afternoon. I present her with the ring and announce that after the wedding we will leave for Rome.

Eve agrees happily. Yesterday we were silent, today we out-talk each other.

I tell her of the orders I have received and share my joy. The portraits must be ready before departure, the copy of the *Jews* I will paint in Rome. On our return to Warsaw, I'll set up a studio and life will be heaven.

In planning these events I promise Eve that the anniversary of yesterday will always be a holiday. But she leans her head on my shoulder and asks me not to speak of it. Then she throws her arms around my neck and calls me her great man. She is paler than usual, her eyes are bluer, but she is simply radiant.

Oh, what an ass I had been having such a woman near, to go looking for happiness somewhere else, in a sphere where I was a stranger and which was foreign to me.

What an artistic nature Eve has. Now that we are engaged, she takes the role seriously and begins to play the part of the happy young fiancée. I cannot hold it against the dear creature who has spent so many years in the theater.

After lunch, we go to visit Helen Kolczanowski.

From the time I am introduced as Eve's fiancé, the prank with the lyrist becomes innocent and causes no disagreement between the ladies. On hearing about the engagement Helen receives me with open arms and rejoices over Eve's good fortune. We laugh like a trio of madmen over what the *lirnik* had to hear about Magorski the painter. Yesterday, I would have stilettoed Ostrzynski, today I admire his wit.

Helen laughs so hard that tears fall from her translu-cent eyes. Speaking aside, she is beautiful. When at the end of the visit she turns her head, both Eve and I are cap-tivated. Eve is so impressed by this mannerism that she unconsciously imitates it, and the look, during the day.

We agree that after our return from abroad I will paint Helen's portrait, but before that I will paint one of my darling Eve. I hope that I can capture those features, so delicate that they are almost ephemeral, and that expres-sive face in which every emotion is reflected like a cloud on calm water.

Sure I can do it, and why not?

The evening *Flyer* carries impossible stories of the commissions I have received. My future income is tallied in the hundreds of thousands.

Perhaps this contributes to the fact that on the follow-ing day I receive a letter from Kathy. She grievously re-grets her rash act of returning the ring in a fit of passion. She says that if I would come over and we would both throw ourselves at the mercy of the parents we would, no doubt, receive forgiveness.

I've had enough of this pleading and throwing at the mercy of. I refuse to answer. Let him who wants to go through all that nonsense. Let Kathy take Ostrzynski, I've got my Eve.

My silence throws the Slusowski camp into a panic.

A few days later a messenger arrives with a letter from Kathy, this time for Swiatecki.

He shows me the letter. Kathy begs that he drop by for a discussion of a matter on which her entire future depends. She says that she is counting on his kind heart and fair disposition which she had noticed at the very first introduction. She pleads for him not to disappoint an unhappy woman. Swiatecki curses, mutters about defenestration and the necessity of hanging parent and progeny at the nearest opportunity, but he goes.

I guess that they will try to influence me through him.

XVIII

Swiatecki, whose heart is soft, has been won over.

He has been at the Slusowskis every night for a week. At home, for the last three days, he has been looking at me in the manner of a wolf surveying his prey.

At the end of the day, just after tea, he spoke to me overtly, "Well, what do you intend to do with that girl?"

"What girl?"

"That…what's her face…Slusowski."

"I'm not going to do anything with her."

A moment of silence follows, then he speaks again, "She cries day after day, I can't stand it anymore."

Oh, what a kind soul.

His voice shakes with emotion, but he clears his throat and adds, "A decent person would not act this way."

"Swiatecki, you begin to remind me of papa Slusowski!"

"It may be, but I'd rather remind you of papa Slusowski than hurt his daughter!"

"Get off my back, will you!"

"Good, I don't even want to know you!"

The conversation ends there and from that moment I am no longer talking to Swiatecki.

We pretend that we don't know each other. What makes it ridiculous is that we continue to live together, have breakfast and tea together, and neither one of us has any intention of moving out.

The date of my wedding approaches.

Through the *Flyer* all Warsaw knows of it. Everyone looks at us, everyone admires Eve. When we visited the exhibit, the throng closed in around us, we had to squeeze our way out.

My anonymous advisoress again sends me letters. She warns me that Eve is not a wife for a man like me.

"I cannot believe what is said about relations between Miss Adami and Mr. Ostrzynski," she writes, "but you, Master, need a wife who would devote everything to your fame and greatness. Miss Adami is an artist herself, she will always want to have things her way."

Swiatecki is still making trips to the Slusowskis. By now he must have assumed the role of consoler, for by now they surely must be aware of my plans.

For Eve I have obtained unlimited leave of absence from the theater. She has begun to comb her hair in a peasant fashion. She wears plain dresses, buttoned to the collar. I must admit that she looks good that way. The scene in the dressing room has not repeated itself. Eve won't let it. At present, I am allowed to kiss her hand. This makes me most anxious, but I consider it a compliment that, after all, I am the one.

She loves me absolutely. We spend entire days together. I have begun to give her drawing lessons.

She is wild about these lessons and painting in general.

XIX

Oh mighty Jove, look down from the dizzy heights of Olympus, things are happening of which philosophers have never dreamed about.

On the eve of my wedding Swiatecki comes to see me. He elbows me and shaking his tousled mop of hair, says gloomily, "Wladek, I have committed a crime."

"Well, now that you have spoken, out with it."

He stares at the floor and speaks as if to himself, "For a drunkard like me, a moral and physical bankrupt to marry a wonderful girl like Kathy is an absolute crime!"

I can't believe my ears. I hug Swiatecki wildly, his protests not withstanding.

The wedding will take place in a few days.

XX

After several months in Rome we receive a sumptuous invitation to the wedding of Mr. Ostrzynski and Helen Turno *primo voto* Kolczanowski.

We cannot go as Eve's health will not permit it.

Eve paints continuously and is making tremendous strides. I received a medal in Pest. A Croatian bourgeois bought the canvas. I have made friends among the painters here.

XXI

My son is born in Verona.

Even Eve admits that she has never seen such a child. Exceptional!

XXII

We have been in Warsaw for a few months now. I have set up the ideal studio.

We visit the Ostrzynski's often. He has sold the Flyer and became the president of a charitable institution which distributes food to unemployed workers. One cannot say anything against his unselfishness or the recognition it brings. He pats my back and calls me generous. He also sponsors literary talents and receives on Wednesdays.

They have no children.

XXIII

Help! I'm dying of laughter.

The Swiateckis have returned from Paris. She poses as the wife of an artist from "Golden Bohemia." He wears silk shirts, longish hair and a Van Dyke beard. I see how she managed to cope with his habits and his character, but how she tamed the jungle on the top of his head will remain a mystery forever.

Swiatecki has not given up "making stiffs," but has branched out into pastoral landscapes. He has had much success. He also does portraits, but is less successful as the flesh tones are reminiscent of his prior works.

I asked him in friendship if he was happy. He answered that he had never dreamed such happiness was possible. I must admit, Kathy far surpassed even my expectations.

And I too would be happy were it not for Eve's failing health. Furthermore, the poor dear is constantly unnerved. I heard her sobbing in the night. I know the cause—she misses the theater. She misses it, but is keeping it welled up.

I started the portrait of Mrs. Helen Ostrzynski. She is an absolutely incomparable woman. Ostrzynski could not stop me from…if it were not for the fact that I love Eve absolutely. If not for this I don't know what would happen.

But I love Eve eternally…eternally…!

COMMENTARY ON THE THIRD ONE

In America those familiar with Henryk Sienkiewicz most likely associate him with *Quo Vadis*,[7] the internationally famous historical novel of persecuted Christians in Nero's Rome. But in Poland he is a beloved prose writer, better known for his *Trilogy*—the three novels: *Ogniem i Mieczem* (*With Fire and Sword*), *Potop* (*The Deluge*), and *Pan Wołodyjowski* (*Colonel Wolodyjowski*).[8]

These three are considered *the* classic historical action adventure stories in Polish literature. Sienkiewicz wrote them to improve the morale of his countrymen after the failure of the insurrection of 1863 and the subsequent repression. Polish society desperately needed a shot in the arm—something to "uplift the hearts." Sienkiewicz provided this and at the same time, almost by accident, wrote a runaway best-seller that developed into the ever popular *Trilogy*.

The formula Sienkiewicz used has been known and repeated since the times of Alexandre Dumas and Walter

---

7   *Quo Vadis* was translated into English at least four times: Jeremiah Curtin—Little Brown and Co.; Boston, 1896; S. A. Binion and S. Malevsky—Grosset and Dunlap; New York, 1897; C. J. Hogarth—Everyman's Library; Dutton, New York, 1941; Wieslaw Kuniczak—Hippocrene Books; New York.

8   The books of the *Trilogy* were originally translated by Jeremiah Curtin and published by Little Brown and Co. in Boston (1886). A more recent, but somewhat controversial, translation is by Wieslaw Kuniczak, Hippocrene Books, New York, 1991-1992.

Scott. A group of three or four skilled warriors, friends sworn to a cause, travel on the far-flung borders of a huge Republic. Their skill at arms is the only law and their natural cleverness the only hope that they will evade their enemies. To move things along there is some comic relief and the occasional lady-fair to rescue. It was not at all different from the format used by George Lucas for his space saga *Star Wars*, except that George freshened up the dueling by giving his heroes "laser sabers" and gravity-defying vehicles in place of horses.

Sienkiewicz was not only a writer of historical action-adventure, he also penned a huge collection of short stories. Best known among these are *Za Chlebem (For Bread)*, *Latarnik (The Lighthouse Keeper)*, and *Janko Muzykant (Janko Musician)*. The plots of these stories are highly melodramatic and conclude with the main characters perishing or, at best, succumbing to the cruel whims of fortune.

In *Za Chlebem*, father and daughter emigrants suffer toil and privation trying to make a new life in the American West. After the father dies, the daughter returns to New York, goes mad and dies of hunger in the street. In *Latarnik* an aging and weary insurrectionist, who had traveled widely and fought in many wars, finally settles into a job as a lighthouse keeper on the California coast. One evening a book of poetry by Adam Mickiewicz, Poland's national bard, is delivered to him. Absorbed in reading, the old man forgets to light the great lantern— and is thrown out of his job to resume the life of a wandering outcast.

In *Janko Muzykant*, a young peasant boy is fascinated by violin music. He cannot hope to obtain such a wonderful instrument for himself but knows that there is one at the nearby manor house. He attempts to steal it, but is caught and given a severe beating for his crime. Weak and emaciated, he dies in his mother's arms.

This last story, required reading in grammar schools, was inflicted upon several generations of Poles by the now defunct communist government. An ideal tool for the authorities in their job of creating a socialist country, it fitted the model for social realism perfectly. A story by a renowned author addressed the theme of injustice and inequality under the class system—a system the new government intended to eliminate in order to bring in the long awaited "bright tomorrow." How could a restrictive government or police state not love an author who supplied ready-made propaganda, even before there was a regime that could make use of it? And so Sienkiewicz's work is endlessly re-purposed and rediscovered by new generations of readers.

Less well known are his other short stories, which are often humorous and laced with pointed social commentary on his times. In all cases the characters are taken from life. For example, the novella *Ta Trzecia (The Third One)*[9] borrows characters freely from among the people who were in Sienkiewicz's circle early during his career.

The plot of the story concerns Wladek Magorski, a painter in late nineteenth century Warsaw who wins the prestigious Salon Prize in Paris for his painting "Jews by the Waters of Babylon." Sudden wealth makes possible his engagement to Kathy Slusowski, the daughter of an ultra-conservative government official. After becoming

---

9   This story was originally translated by Jeremiah Curtin and published by Little Brown and Co. Boston (1897) in a story collection entitled *Hania* (after one of the stories). This earlier text may be downloaded for free from Google Books on the Internet.

engaged, Wladek is distracted by the appearance of Helen, a beautiful and wealthy Ukrainian widow. Because of his sudden and undeserved reputation as a "Don Juan," he is unable to obtain a "proper" introduction to the lady. With the help of his long-time actress friend Eve Adami, he disguises himself as an elderly Ukrainian *lirnik* (lyrist) and plays and sings for the beautiful Helen. The subterfuge is exposed by his rival, the journalist Ostrzynski, who writes about the "mysterious Ukrainian bard" in a newspaper gossip column. As the situation careens out of control, Wladek discovers that he is actually in love with Eve. The rejected Kathy pairs up with Wladek's roommate Anthony Swiatecki, while Helen marries Ostrzynski. They would all live happily ever after except that Eve has bouts of illness—possibly tuberculosis—and misses the excitement of her stage career.

Any one of the Polish "Young Poland" movement painters could have served as a model for Wladek Magorski, the main character in the story, as well as for his close friend Anthony Swiatecki, but it was painter Józef Chełmoński who actually donned Ukrainian folk costume in order to pursue a romantic liaison. The engagement between Wladek and Kathy had its roots in the author's unfortunate relationship with Maria Keller.

The Keller family of Warsaw was part of the bourgeois establishment, with strict Victorian morals and a materialistic outlook. Young Henryk, having close ties to the bohemian community of writers, painters, and actors was very much an outsider in this society. Eventually, he was sent packing by his intended's father because of his poor earning potential. Little did the family know, to their certain regret, that this would change in the not-so-distant future. Sienkiewicz no doubt captured the family's stodgy attitudes well and described them precisely—as snobs and philistines—with but a few small modifications. Where Kathy's father's position is given as being in the government's treasury department, his actual prospective father-in-law was an upper-level functionary of the post office.

The actress in the story, Eve Adami, is modeled on the queen of nineteenth century Polish theater—Helena Modrzejewska. Meanwhile, Helen the wealthy Ukrainian beauty appears as an actual person mentioned in a letter that Modrzejewska sent to Sienkiewicz sometime during his stay in America.

Incidentally, Sienkiewicz was in the United States to find a place where Modrzejewska, her husband, and son could start a communal farm. In this venture they were to be joined by a group of artists from Poland. They eventually settled in Anaheim, California, but the experiment in combining farming and art eventually wilted. Within a year, however, Modrzejewska learned English well enough to perform on the American stage. She changed her name to Modjeska and started an entirely new career, one that made her both an international star of the stage and a legend in Poland.

She wrote[10] the following to Henryk Sienkiewicz shortly before her departure from Warsaw for the sunny shores of California, about June 15, 1876.

Henryk!
    We are getting closer to the day of our departure; every day we relieve ourselves of a few more items from

10 The letter is from *Korespondencja Heleny Modrzejewskiej i Karola Chłapowskiego*, edited by Jerzy Got and Józef Szczublewski, Vol. 1, Warsaw, 1965; Letter 170, p. 3; translation by P. Obst.

the apartment, selling out quickly, but we won't be able to leave before the middle of July, because the wife of Julek [Sypniewski] has fooled herself and us: the expected arrival of the descendant [birth of their child] has not yet happened and it appears not anxious to get out into the world. Perhaps it is afraid of the forthcoming voyage and is in hiding. [My husband] Karol is in desperation because of this, and it's not convenient for me either to stretch out the departure, especially since the apartment will be taken on July 1. Ha! In my sorrow I will go to Lwów to perform [she gave guest performances in Lwów from June 26 to the first days of July 1876]. Maria Deryng was hired to play in my place for a very small salary—1200 reis schillings and 5 reis schillings for expenses per. Their family will be living in awful poverty for a year.

You have not written about the way the locality looks, while here Witkiewicz is continually sketching out the farm, to show [in layout] the house, barn and alfalfa without end, and walking among it—ten people with parasols. I trust it's not that bad? And even if it were, then it's all the same—all I want is some peace.

I had news from Paris. [Józef Marian] Chełmoński as you well know, had a tremendous success selling two of his paintings for 18,000 franks, and Matylda [Godebska] writes that he did change a bit—became more civilized. Though from his last letter I cannot detect any great changes. He keeps writing in verse. Lately his poems, because of our forthcoming departure, sound as follows:

On the Black Sea a diver collects beads
and places them on translucent leads,
It's neither wax nor precious amber,
I love you, but you wander.... etc. etc.

You have no idea how the tongues are wagging here, how many commentaries are made on our voyage, and nobody knows anything in detail. Sometimes I find them entertaining, but this talk is more often boring and I wish to make an exit as soon as possible.

I don't know if Karol has told you that my mother will not go with us. It is a great sorrow to me, but we cannot expose her to the hardships of such a long voyage. I don't know if Sonatka [?] will go or not—perhaps her parents will not allow her to go. But, wait! There's a rich lady from Ukraine who has fallen in love with you, seeing only your photograph from Niagara, and now she will give me no peace. She reads your articles as if they were holy writ and tells me about them; she exults over Hania [one of Sienkiewicz's novellas] and in every way tortures me so that I would arrange a marriage for her with you. I promised her that I will introduce her to you on my return—but I doubt if you would take a liking to her. She asks me why you should not like her? I answer: "Look, here's a man who goes out to hunt tigers; do you think he will fall for any girl?" She shakes when I say this then sighs and becomes silent.

Janek Komierowski [an amateur singer] was happy that you mentioned him in your letter. I wanted to marry him off to the above-mentioned lady, but I was not successful. He promised to search through your desk most diligently, and then write about the result of the search.

Till we meet again, Henryk! Write again, quickly!

I clasp your hands. Helena

This is one of a few surviving letters from Helena Modrzejewska to Henryk Sienkiewicz. By her own admission Modrzejewska burned all the letters she received from Sienkiewicz, leading some to speculate there had been a romantic relationship between the two. If there was, the infatuation did not last long, but they did remain life-long friends. Sienkiewicz was married three times and had two children—a son and a daughter. He also knew well the pains and tribulations of being a fiancé. He ended one romantic relationship with a declaration of "brotherly and spiritual love" for the lady. By a convenient coincidence all three of the women he married were named Maria—making it nearly impossible for him to utter the wrong name in a moment of passion.

Wladek's rival Ostrzynski came from the world of editors who staffed the many competing periodicals published in Warsaw. Sienkiewicz himself was an editor at *Słowo (Word)*, and eventually quit the job in disgust.

As the romantic agitations of the principals in *The Third One* build to a climax, Sienkiewicz discharges the tension through the medium of the newspaper gossip column. Ostrzynski exposes the identity of the Ukrainian lyrist but at the same time protects the popular actress Eve Adami from public censure. He makes Magorski out to be a fool in front of his admirers by ending the article with: "The old bard apparently marched here straight from Ukraine. His reason is dim, though his memory is excellent...."

Fans of 1950s era films may notice vague parallels in this story and the script of the enormously popular Joseph Mankiewicz film *All About Eve*. In both stories Eve is a stage actress and there are romantic complications, an acid-tongued theater critic, and most importantly, the plot pivots on gossip column commentary. In the film's introductory narration, Mankiewicz even mentions the actress Helena Modjeska. It should be added that he took home two *Oscars* for this film—for writing and direction. Some later commented that the reason God gave Mankiewicz two hands was so he could hold both statuettes at once.

In this he eclipsed his older brother Herman, who only received one Academy Award—for writing the script to Orson Welles' *Citizen Kane*.

After the furor produced by the article dies down, the characters in both stories find their true loves and chart their futures. The ending of *The Third One* tapers out to an almost-blissful existence for all three pairs of lovers, with but one fly in the ointment: Eve misses her theater career and has bouts of illness.

The illness is not unlike that suffered by Sienkiewicz's first wife, which ended in her death from tuberculosis. The story, however, remains open ended. Was there going to be a sequel? Were Eve and Wladek to have more romantic comedy adventures? It certainly is a possibility. Other Sienkiewicz stories had sequels, and after all, *Gone with the Wind*, the great American novel, is open ended. The question most often asked—"Will Rhett and Scarlett ever be reunited?"—went unanswered for many years. When it finally was addressed in the television mini-series *Scarlett* (1994), the result was most unsatisfactory. Perhaps some questions about certain characters' futures should remain unanswered.

Sienkiewicz's writing is so vivid and animated that many of his stories were reimagined for the screen. The entire *Trilogy* was filmed, creating what historian Norman Davies called "the ultimate Eastern Western." Though the films tended to be rather long—*The Deluge (Potop)* alone runs a daunting (and arse numbing) 5 hours 15 minutes in the full-length version[11]—they were very popular with audiences all over the world because of their lively

---

11 The filmed version of *The Deluge* was made in Poland in 1974 by Jerzy Hoffman. It received a nomination for an Academy Award, Best Foreign Language Film, but did not win.

duels and battle sequences. *Quo Vadis* was made as a film several times: initially silent (1913), then in the 1950s as a Cinemascope sword and sandal Hollywood epic with Robert Taylor and Deborah Kerr, and later by the Poles in a more cerebral but somewhat disjointed version.[12]

The Third One is ideally suited for translation to the screen. When gratuitous violence and mindless explosions are the rule by which Hollywood measures achievement in the cinematic arts, it may be a time for relief in a return to witty dialogue and clashes of personalities, like the ones found in the best films of Hollywood's "Romantic Comedy" era.

---

12 A Polish film version of *Quo Vadis* was made by Jerzy Kawalerowicz in 2001. It was the most expensive Polish film production ever made, but was not a box-office success. More information about this and other filmed versions of Sienkiewicz stories may be found through the Internet Movie Data Base (www.imdb.com).

A SIENKIEWICZ FILMOGRAPHY

COMPLIED FROM INTERNET MOVIE DATA BASE AND OTHER SOURCES

QUO VADIS

Quo Vadis (2001) color DVD
> 274 min - Drama - 14 September 2001 (Poland)
> Director: Jerzy Kawalerowicz
> Writers: Jerzy Kawalerowicz, Henryk Sienkiewicz (novel)
> Stars: Pawel Delag, Magdalena Mielcarz, Boguslaw Linda
> Production co: Chronos-Film, Home Box Office (HBO), Kredyt Bank PBI S.A.
> Note: film was never shown on cable television in United States

Quo Vadis? (1985) color DVD
> TV Mini-Series - 360 min - Drama (Italy - International Production)
> Series Directed by: Franco Rossi
> Stars: Klaus Maria Brandauer, Frederic Forrest, Cristina Raines
> Production co: Rai Uno Radiotelevisione, Leone Film, Antenne-2

Quo Vadis (1951) color DVD
> 171 min - Drama - Romance - 25 December 1951
> (USA)
> Director: Mervyn LeRoy
> Writers: John Lee Mahin (screenplay), S.N. Behrman
> (screenplay)
> Stars: Robert Taylor, Deborah Kerr, Leo Genn, Peter
> Ustinov
> Production co: Metro-Goldwyn-Mayer (MGM),
> Loew's

The Sign of the Cross (1932) DVD b/w
> 108 min - Drama - History
> Director: Cecil B. DeMille
> Writers: Waldemar Young (screen play), Sidney
> Buchman (screen play)
> Stars: Fredric March, Elissa Landi, Claudette Colbert,
> Charles Laughton
> Production co: Paramount Pictures
> Note: version of Quo Vadis not credited to Henryk
> Sienkiewicz but the story source is obvious

Quo Vadis? (1925) b/w
> 90 min - Drama - Silent - 1925 (Italy)
> Directors: Gabriellino D'Annunzio, Georg Jacoby
> Writers: Gabriellino D'Annunzio, Georg Jacoby
> Stars: Emil Jannings, Elena Sangro, Rina De Liguoro
> Production co: Unione Cinematografica Italiana

Quo Vadis? (1913) b/w
> 120 min - Drama - History - Silent - 1913 (Italy)
> Director: Enrico Guazzoni
> Writers: Henryk Sienkiewicz (novel), Enrico
> Guazzoni
> Stars: Amleto Novelli, Gustavo Serena, Amelia

Cattaneo
Production co: Societe Italiana Cines
Note: The first movie to run for two hours.

Quo Vadis? (original title)
a.k.a. *Whence Does He Come?* (1901) b/w - silent
(France)
1 min - Short Subject
Directors: Lucien Nonguet, Ferdinand Zecca
Writer: Henryk Sienkiewicz (novel)
Production co: Pathe Freres

THE TRILOGY

With Fire and Sword (1999) color DVD
"Ogniem i mieczem" (original title)
175 min - Adventure - Drama - (Poland)
Director: Jerzy Hoffman
Writers: Jerzy Hoffman, Henryk Sienkiewicz (novel)
Stars: Izabella Scorupco, Michal Zebrowski,
Aleksandr Domogarov
Production co: Agencja Produkcji Filmowej,
Kredyt Bank PBI S.A. (I), Okocimskie Zaklady
Piwowarskie S.A.

The Deluge (1974) color DVD
"Potop" (original title)
315 min - Adventure, History, Romance - (Poland)
Director: Jerzy Hoffman
Writers: Jerzy Hoffman, Adam Kersten
Stars: Daniel Olbrychski, Malgorzata Braunek,
Tadeusz Lomnicki
Production co: A.P. Dovzenko Filmstudio,
Belarusfilm, PRF "Zespol Filmowy"

Colonel Wolodyjowski (1969)
  "Pan Wolodyjowski" (original title) color DVD
  160 min - Adventure - (Poland)
  Director: Jerzy Hoffman
  Writers: Jerzy Hoffman, Jerzy Lutowski
  Stars: Tadeusz Lomnicki, Magdalena Zawadzka,
    Mieczyslaw Pawlikowski
  Production co: Film Polski, Zespol Filmowy
    "Kamera"

Invasion 1700 a.k.a. *Daggers of Blood* (1962) DVD color
  "Col ferro e col fuoco" (original title) based on
    "Ogniem i Mieczem"
  112 min - Action, Adventure, Drama - Italy, France,
    Yugoslavia
  Director: Fernando Cerchio
  Writers: Henryk Sienkiewicz (novel), Ugo Liberatore
  Stars: John Drew Barrymore, Jeanne Crain, Pierre
    Brice, Elena Zareschi
  Production co: Avala Film, Comptoir Francais du Film
    Production (CFFP), FilmEuropa
  Note: Taormina International Film Festival 1962
    Director prize Golden Charybdis

Flood (1915) b/w silent; *"Potop"* (original title) (Russia)
  Director: Pyotr Chardynin
  Writer: Henryk Sienkiewicz (novel)
  Stars: Aleksandr Kheruvimov, Pavel Knorr, Ivan
    Mozzhukhin

Obrona czestochowy [*Defense of Czestochowa*] (1913)
b/w silent
  Drama, History - (Poland)
  Director: Edward Puchalski
  Writers: Edmund Michrowski (screenplay), Henryk

Sienkiewicz (novel)
Stars: Maria Duleba, Aleksander Zelwerowicz, Stefan
    Jaracz
Production co: Sokol
Note: Based on "Potop"

IN DESERT AND WILDERNESS

W pustyni i w puszczy [*In Desert and Wilderness*] (2002)
color
TV Mini-Series - 45 min - Adventure, Drama, Family
    (Poland)
Stars: Adam Fidusiewicz, Konrad Imiela, Mzwandile
    Ngubeni
Production co: Telewizja Polska (TVP), Vision Film
    Production

In Desert and Wilderness (2001) DVD color
    "W pustyni i w puszczy" (original title)
    111 min - (Poland)
    Director: Gavin Hood
    Writers: Gavin Hood, Henryk Sienkiewicz (novel)
    Stars: Adam Fidusiewicz, Karolina Sawka, Artur
        Zmijewski

W pustyni i w puszczy [*In Desert and Wilderness*] (1974)
    TV Mini-Series - 200 min - Adventure (Poland)
    Stars: Edmund Fetting, Stanislaw Jasiukiewicz,
        Tomasz Medrzak
    Note: Edited from "W pustyni i w puszczy" (1973)

W pustyni i w puszczy [*In Desert and Wilderness*]
   1973)
195 min - 15 October 1973 (Poland)
Director: Wladyslaw Slesicki
Writers: Henryk Sienkiewicz (novel), Wladyslaw
   Slesicki
Stars: Monika Rosca, Tomasz Medrzak, Edmund
   Fetting

NOVELS AND NOVELLAS

Hania (1984)
   TV Movie - 87 min - Drama, Romance - 3 June 1984
      (Poland)
   Directors: Krzysztof Wierzbianski, Stanislaw Wohl
   Writers: Jozef Hen, Henryk Sienkiewicz (novel)
   Stars: Tadeusz Bartosik, Jan Englert, Barbara
      Horawianka
   Production co: Studio Filmowe Perspektywa

Black Cross [*The Teutonic Knights*] (1960) color DVD
   "Krzyzacy" (original title)
   166 min - Adventure, Drama, History - (Poland)
    Director: Aleksander Ford
   Writers: Aleksander Ford (dialogue), Aleksander Ford
      (screenplay)
   Stars: Urszula Modrzynska, Grazyna Staniszewska,
      Andrzej Szalawski
   Production co: Zespol Filmowy "Studio"

Szkice weglem [*Charcoal Sketches*] (1957) b/w
   92 min - 25 November 1957 (Poland)
   Director: Antoni Bohdziewicz
   Writers: Henryk Sienkiewicz (story), Ariadna

Demkowska
Stars: Wieslaw Golas, Stanislaw Bareja, Stefan Bartik
Production co: P.P. Film Polski

Janko Muzykant (1930) b/w
70 min - Poland (USA)
Director: Ryszard Ordynski
Writers: Ferdynand Goetel, Henryk Sienkiewicz (short
    story)
Stars: Stefan Rogulski, Witold Conti, Maria Malicka
Production co: Blok-Muzafilm

Bartek zwyciezca [*Bartek the Victor*] (1923) b/w
Drama - 4 November 1923 (Poland)
Director: Edward Puchalski
Writers: Edward Puchalski, Henryk Sienkiewicz
    (novel)
Stars: Wladyslaw Pytlasinski, Eugenia Zasempianka,
    Roman Zelazowski
Production co: Poznanska Wytwornia Filmowa

Na jasnym brzegu [*On the Bright Shore*] 1921) b/w silent
Drama, Romance - 25 December 1921 (Poland)
Director: Edward Puchalski
Writers: Henryk Sienkiewicz (novel), Adam Zagorski
Stars: Maria Korska, Aleksandra Cwikiewicz, Jozef
    Sliwicki
Production co: Ornak
    Anna [*Hania*] (1920) b/w silent
July 1920 (Italy)
Director: Giuseppe de Liguoro
Writer: Henryk Sienkiewicz (story)
Stars: Guido Trento, Cecyl Tryan
Production co: Gladiator Film

Krwawa dola [*Bloody Fate*] (1912) b/w silent
    Drama - 14 May 1912 (Poland)
    Director: Wladyslaw Palinski
    Writer: Henryk Sienkiewicz (short story "Szkice
        weglem")
    Stars: Maria Mirska, Antoni Bednarczyk, Aniela
        Boguslawska
    Production co: Kooperatywa Artystyczna

DOCUMENTARY

Henryk Sienkiewicz w Oblegorku (1916) b/w silent
    Documentary - Short - (Poland)
    Director: Jan Skarbek-Malczewski
    Stars: Henryk Sienkiewicz
    Production co: Sfinks